W9-AUD-999

JOY SCHOOL

Elizabeth Berg

JOY SCHOOL

Published in Large Print by arrangement with Random House, Inc. in the United States and Canada.

Wheeler Large Print Book Series.

Set in 16 pt Plantin.

Library of Congress Cataloging-in-Publication Data

Berg, Elizabeth.
Joy school / Elizabeth Berg.
p. (large print) cm.(Wheeler large print book series)
sequel to: Durable Goods
ISBN 1-56895-488-3 (hardcover)
1. Large type books.
I. Title. II. Series
[PS3552.E6996J69 1997]
813′.54—dc21 97-034311
CIP

For Marianne Quasha,
Whose stories inspire me
And whose friendship sustains me,
and for Billy Young,
Charming, patient and true.

This time I want first to acknowledge those readers who have taken the trouble to write and tell me how they feel about my books. Your letters live in a beautiful brown box and are cherished.

And thanks again to my writing group; to my agent, Lisa Bankoff, and her assistant, Abigail Rose, and to my editor, Kate Medina, and her assistant, Renana Meyers. Thanks also to Alfred Connell, landlord *extraordinaire*, who rents me my beautiful office in the great town of Natick, and to Buzzy Bartone, an artist whose medium is flowers, and whose work brings everyone joy.

JOY SCHOOL

The housekeeper is ironing and I am lying on the floor beside her, trying to secretly look up her dress. I can't see anything but her slip. It is white, a skinny line of lace trim on the bottom, which I already knew because it was hanging out when she first got here, snowing down south. I had a thought to tell her, in a nice way. But what would be the point, it's only us two here and I'm not offended.

I used to think you had to be rich to have a housekeeper, but it's not true. Sometimes you are rich, but sometimes you only have a need and that is when you get messy housekeepers like this one. Not that I don't like her. Ginger is her name, like the dancer, and her hair is blond like that dancer, too. She wears socks that fall down into the backs of her loafers—thin, white, wrong ones, though she is done with school so it isn't so important. I found out at my new high school, where I am a freshman, about wrong socks and I had to quit wearing them. Of course that is only the tip of the iceberg.

Ginger takes the bus here. She carries a bag made out of rough striped material with wooden handles, and in the bag are slippers and her lunch and a paperback book with a curled-up cover which she reads every day at noontime. Once she gave me the candy bar from her lunch. Oh no, I said but she said, Oh sure, go ahead, I don't need it. It was the Hershey's with almonds kind. Usually she has Heath, so I think it was a case of this was a substitute candy bar anyway, so I did take it. I ate it that night while I read in bed with my knees up. This is how my mother did it, only she also ate fruit. I don't like fruit unless it is hot and in a pie. I suppose that is un-American and another thing wrong with me, which it seems is all that is happening now is I am finding out everything wrong with me. This place and I do not get along.

Ginger shifts a little on her feet, and the slip moves and now I can see her underpants. They are only white. I get up and go into my room and close the door quietly so as not to hurt her feelings. I mean that she can't come in, but it's not anything against her.

I take out the letter from my drawer. It still smells of lilacs. She'd drawn a circle on the envelope, saying, "Sniff here!" but I didn't have to smell that place, the whole letter smelled.

Dear Katie,
I have been so unbelievably busy and that's why it has taken so long to write to you. I like your letters. They're funny.

The family that moved into your house is useless. There are only little kids and the parents are all the time asking me to baby-sit, which I do NOT have time for. As if I wanted to even if I did have time. I believe I am done with baby-sitting. Even though last time at McLaughlin's you would not believe what I found, I looked in their dresser drawer and found a box of rubbers!!!! You remember when Marybeth told us she had seen a weenie because when her parents weren't home that time Jerry Southerland had come out of her bathroom with it hanging out (DON'T let ANYONE see this letter!!!!!!!) and it was all red at the tip like a dog's? Well, I saw that box of rubbers and I was thinking how it would look on the red and you can imagine how I wanted to puke.

But anyway. I am class president this year and there are so many serious responsibilities. I just found out last week, we had elections. I thought I would win, but I didn't know. We are going to have lots of dances. First the Snow Ball. So I am busy. I have already given two speeches in front of the whole class and you know you have to practice a LOT for that kind of thing because you are setting the whole tone.

I am right now pulling out an eyelash to send to you because I miss you, too. Keep writing to me and also you can send poetry, but maybe not so many at a time. Have you found a boyfriend yet? I think your life could be much better with one of those. That is something every woman needs full time.

Well, my mother is calling me to set the table. Like I could care. See you soon. Well, not see you!!!! But, you know what I mean.

Love,

Cherylanne

I look at the clock on my desk. Seven after three. Nothing to do. Saturday afternoon, the hours stretching out like railroad tracks across the desert. I am tired of reading. It is dangerous to take a walk, since my enemies live across the street and they are all the time watching for me. I wish I could take a nap, like a baby. I lie down, close my eyes.

I'm not tired.

I turn on my side, put my thumb in my mouth. It feels like it's forty times the size it really is. It used to feel so comfortable, like there was a satiny pocket in my mouth for it to slide into. I take my thumb out, wipe it on my shirt, turn onto my back and stare at the whorls on my ceiling. Here is my white sky. It will become my next poem, which I will call "The Absence of Blue." *White sky,* I think. And then I think nothing.

The beginning is always so hard. Any beginning is always so hard.

I hear a knock at my door, then Ginger's voice saying, "Katie? I have some blouses here for you."

I sit up, straighten the spread beside me. Well, good. A visitor. And when my father comes home, we're going to McDonald's, he already said. I line my feet up beside each other, push my hair neater under my headband. "Come in," I say, in a high and cultured voice like I am rich and living in England in my own walk-up apartment. I will think of something to ask Ginger so that her answer will be long and interesting.

She comes in, hangs my blouses up. I can see the outline of her bra through the back of her blouse. She is a grown-up woman. "Ginger," I say. "Can I ask you something?"

She turns around. "You just did."

"Right," I say, smiling, and then, "I mean, something else. A personal thing."

Her face changes, and in it I see a little fear. Like maybe she thinks since I'm the daughter I could fire her. I want to say, "Did you ever have any trouble in school with kids being kind of mean to you? If so, what did you do about it?" Like an essay question. But when I start to ask, all that comes out is, "Did you like high school?"

She sits down beside me, lightly touches my hair. "Oh, honey," she says, a faraway look in her eyes like the girls in the romance comic books, "I loved school. These are the best years of your life."

"Oh," I say. "Uh-huh." I hope not, I'm thinking. I sure hope not.

"Is that what you wanted to ask?"

"Yes," I say. Never mind.

"Well," she says, "that's not so personal."

"No."

"I was thinking I'd make some peanut-butter cookies," she says, slow and careful. I nod. It seems to me that we always have our antennae out, no matter what we say; that we can pick up on a person's hurt in our hearts even if it never makes it to our brains. And people like Ginger have the manners to do something about it. I will get to mash every raw cookie with the fork to make the crisscross pattern. You feel a little talented when you see the cookies come out of the oven. Ginger lets me do all the good parts, every time. Pretty soon, I could love her.

Here is my life, five days a week. First off, English. Mrs. Brady. She is actually my favorite, so I wish I didn't have her first, I wish she would be saved to make up for the rest of the day. But she is first. She has a beehive hairdo, and when she stands by the window, you can see through it. It sort of looks like brown cotton candy. Once I saw a hairpin coming out a little and that is what reminded me that her hair isn't always like that. She has black cat-eye glasses, and she always wears this outfit: a pleated skirt, a blouse with usually a round collar, a cardigan sweater, brown shoes with heels so little you don't know they're heels until she turns around to write on the blackboard. Her handwriting is so clear and beautiful. I can't believe a person does it. Even on the board, every letter so perfect, every line so straight. She was born to be a teacher, you can tell by everything she does, including walking across the room talking to us but also deep in thought. She is serious about her subject and she says things that are heartfelt and she doesn't care who makes fun of her in the halls afterward. Especially poetry. When she reads from the skinny books she brings in, she'll speak so hard from her feelings that her voice gets deeper. And when she's done, she'll press the open book into herself, just under her bosom.

The pages must get warm from her body heat. Sometimes I think of her and her husband sitting at their kitchen table eating dinner, their napkins exact squares on their laps, talking in prayer voices about John Keats. About the tragedy of how he died, looking out the window in a foreign place, thinking, oh jeez, it didn't get to happen. Maybe they eat by candlelight while the hi-fi plays piano music—it wouldn't surprise me at all. It would be so cute, how the light of the flames would flicker in their eyeglasses when they were being so serious.

Mrs. Brady calls on me when no one else gets it, even if my hand is not up. This is how I know that in a way I am her pet. I think in a tidy corner of her brain she keeps the thought, Well, I can always count on Katie. And she is right. There is nothing in English so far that I don't like, even the sonnets that I have never heard of anyone else liking except English teachers. I excel in English, I always have. Not the grammar part, but getting what the author means. Interpretation, they call it. I think it's why I got to skip grade four.

After English comes the opposite: Math. Harry Hadd is the teacher, if you can imagine such a name. He wears a wrinkly white shirt and no tie and some pants that look like one little breeze through the window and they'll fall down. His shoes are black high-top sneakers, except for a day when the principal came to watch the class. Then he wore brown tie shoes all shined up fake. He keeps his sleeves rolled up and it is a mystery to him why every kid in class does not understand everything in the book from day one. He says things like that all the time, "day one." He calls us by our last names, too, "Miss Woodward," "Mr. Evans." This makes us all feel worse. They have tracks here in this school, and I believe I am in the dumbest class for math. It's supposed to be a big secret, but give me a break. Everybody knows. In English I'm in with the smart kids. They mostly have all their classes together. I only do well in English. In other subjects I am normal except in math where I am dismal. In those achievement tests you have to take, my line for math goes so far down, way below the red line they draw in that says you should at least be here. I just don't get math. Even if I go for extra help, one on one, I don't get it. I went for a lot of extra help in another school, where I had a teacher who was so nice, Mr. Dieter. He was a real ugly man married to such a pretty woman, which always made me in a good mood. He would explain and explain and explain and it was like my brain was closed for business. Finally, I would just feel so sorry for him I would say, Oh! I get it! but I never did. And he would hand me back my D- test with a small red note, "Katie—what happened? See me."

Third period, gym. If I were to make up a torture for someone, it would be you have to have gym right in the middle of your day. Your body is not in the mood for gym in the middle of the day. You have done some work to try to look all right for the day, you have slept on rollers and stood in front of your mirror for a long while that morning and all that, and then splat, gym. You have to run around and get messed up and then you have to take a shower and even if you cheat and just stand in front of it with your towel on, your underwear hidden beneath, the steam still gets you. And changing in front of everyone. And smelling that rubbery smell mixed with BO. Plus the teacher, as usual, is a mean woman. Every gym teacher I've ever had has been mean, like she has a problem she is going to punish all of us for out on the courts. This gym teacher is named Miss Sweet. This would be what they call irony, I'll tell you that. Even though she is called Miss Sweat behind her back. She has little lips, which you think the body forgot to send the bloodline to; they are pale and straight. She wears gym shorts and a sweatshirt with the sleeves pushed up and severe socks and sneakers. They're the same gym shorts we wear, but on her they look different. She has a whistle around her neck, and her hair is pulled back into a ponytail although it's not long enough for one. It's like she's so strict even her hair cannot be loose. She carries around a clipboard to write mean things down about you, and once when I failed to clear the bar for the high jump, she hit me on the butt with it. It was because in her opinion I should have been able to do it. I tried again, failed again, but she didn't hit me again because I wasn't worth it. If I ever get to be God, I'm calling all the gym teachers in the world into one room to say this: All right, knock it off!! And then I'm going to make them all change into pink formals with pink satin heels. If I were to draw on a paper what gym does for me, I would make one dot. And then I would erase it. But I have to do it, every day, in the middle of the day, right before lunch.

Which is another thing.

It is hard enough to do lunch when you know a place. But when you are new, you have never seen anything so big as the lunchroom. There are secret maps, and you'd better not mess up. Which I did, of course. The first day, I sat at the popular table. As if I should know. First one perfect girl sat down, then another. They were making big eyes at one another, rattling their bracelets around, but nobody said anything. They just sat around me like white surrounding black until I got it. I said, "Excuse me," and moved, and they all laughed together. It was kind of a pretty sound.

I sit mostly by myself, or by someone miscellaneous. I don't talk. At first I tried, but nothing good ever came of it. I would see the person I'd talked to in the hall the next day and say hi and they would look at me like, *What?* So I just eat and that is the one good thing about this school, they have very good food. On Sloppy Joe day, I go back for seconds. I get them, too. The cafeteria ladies like me. They see what goes on. Kids think they stand back there with their big metal spoons and big aprons and just think, Oh I see the corn has gone down, I guess I'll go on back and get some more. But when you look up you see that of course all the faces are different. And they are interested in you and friendly and a lot of them really care that you eat well. And they feel happy when you like things. They don't usually give seconds, especially not to the boys, who are not sincere when they ask, who just want to use seconds for food fights. But they will give more to me. This is how far things have gone down, that my only friends in school are the cafeteria ladies. And not even really. They take breaks together, they sit at a table in the corner with some coffee and a little of this and a little of that, things we had for lunch. If I went up and sat with them, they wouldn't like it either. I think in about a few months I will be sitting with someone real. It's hard to tell. I have never had such a hard time getting my place in a school. You wish you could bring a book of directions to yourself that everyone would read. But no. You just have to wait until the time that a crack comes.

After lunch is history. This man who teaches it, Mr. Spurlock, is insane. Here is his idea of how to teach: Copy notes that you have written in your bent-up spiral notebook onto the blackboard. Tell the class to shut up about two hundred times. Write small and creepy so nobody can read it. Then tell your class to copy the notes from the board into their notebooks. While they do, sit at your desk and read the newspaper and pick at your side teeth with your little finger. Just before the bell rings, say, "Any questions?" I swear this is exactly true. Not one kid likes him. Plus his shoes are about five hundred years old. If he were mental, which his shoes look like, you would feel sorry for him. But he is not mental. He is just the worst teacher of all time in the history of the whole universe. Probably he is a made-up thing from a science experiment to find out: How much can kids take?

Next, French, and the teacher is so beautiful she could be Miss America. She wears French things like a scarf around her neck. She wears short-sleeved sweaters and long tight skirts and nice leather shoes that tie. She smells like good perfume. But her problem is that she never speaks English to us and sometimes we just need to know something. It is only beginning French. So what I want to know is where does she get off from the first day rattling on in French, French, French? One day I tried to complain. After class. I said, "Miss Worthington, I don't think you should talk only in French." And she said, "Ah, ah, ah! *En français!!*" You feel wound-up frustrated in there. But here is the most surprising thing: I am learning French. Last Saturday, when the mailman came, I said, *"Voici le facteur!"* My father asked me What did I say and I said That was French for Here's the mailman, and he said Is that right? So at home I am glad I have her. But in class it is a torture. Sometimes in class I see that my heel is jiggling bad.

Last in the day is home ec. Here is where they teach you how to make food you never want to eat and how to make clothes you never want to wear. Our menu for Fall Festival will be pork-sausage casserole. It has sweet potatoes and apples in it. The teacher's name is Miss Woods and every time I see her I think about a woman who got colored wrong in the coloring book. She has really red hair, from a box, anyone can see. She wears way too much blusher and blue eye shadow. My best friend Cherylanne lives in Texas, where I just moved from last summer, and she knows everything about makeup. But I know she would throw up her hands in despair if she was told to fix this woman. Miss Woods talks in a high, excited voice and she hardly ever shuts up. I guess one good thing I could say about her is she is always in a good mood. We're going to make aprons next week out of dishcloths.

And that's school, except for the bus ride and homeroom. Homeroom is where they vote for people to be things and where the crabby teacher takes attendance. Every day, she looks like she has just been in a fight. And we are supposed to go to her with problems. She is our advisor. Here is her advice: Don't bug me. And the bus ride? Imagine you are alone on a bumpy vehicle that smells like baloney and takes ten hours to go one block. That is it.

There is a routine on Saturday morning. First, my father sleeps late. I clean my room and then come into the kitchen to plan dinner, because that is my night to cook. I am good at meat loaf and baking whole things like a chicken. He doesn't care if we have repeats, so this morning I am thinking I'll just make meat loaf like I did last week. But when I sit down to eat cereal and look at my cookbook I find the recipe for Italian spaghetti and think maybe I'll try that. It looks good all curled up on the plate. They also show you some bread sticks in a glass in the middle of the table and the tablecloth is red-and-white checkered. This is what my home ec teacher would call setting the scene. She'd probably tell you to play some Italian accordion music on the hi-fi, too. This cookbook is for kids and the first instruction is always this: Wash your hands. Like they're talking to morons. I've outgrown it. But there are still some good ideas in it.

The spaghetti recipe says you have to use tomato sauce and tomato paste and Italian seasoning, which I don't think we have. So I will have to wait until he wakes up to go to the store and get some. I kind of like getting ingredients you don't have at home to make something. That puts you even more in the mood to make it. I wish I could go to the store myself, but nothing is walking distance from here except a church at the end of the block. It's Catholic. It has a very quiet smell of incense all the time, which is nice, and it has very pretty windows, the stained-glass kind where the red looks like wine and the blue is so deep and beautiful you wish you could put it in your pocket and take it home with you. I like to sit in that church when no one is there, although I do sit in the back row, since we're not members. The cushions are a dark-red velvet that turns lighter if you rub it the wrong way. Sometimes I kneel there, not to pray, just to make my head that kind of empty still that has a person feel more comfortable than they thought they were. The priest there is named Father Compton. He doesn't mind my being there. He calls you "child" like he's in the movies. He's old and has whole tufts of white hair growing out of his nose and he walks bent over, but his eyes are clear and smart and they notice the right things. When he's looking at you, you can tell he's thinking kind thoughts, but he doesn't embarrass you by saying them out loud. You don't have to do anything back.

I am washing out my cereal bowl when the phone rings. I answer it quickly and there is my sister, Diane. It is such a miracle to hear her. I haven't heard her voice since we moved here nearly six months ago. I hold the receiver so still, like she could fall out of it if I'm not careful. I feel tears start in my eyes, I'm so glad to hear her. "Where are you?" I say.

"Mexico. I'm still here. But listen, I'm coming to visit you!"

"You are?" I will have to wake him up to give her directions.

"Yes. For Thanksgiving."

"And Dickie?"

"Yeah, he'll come. He'll bring me." I hear the hidden sigh in her voice. She always seems to run into sadness. But when you hear that sound in her voice, if you ask her what's wrong she will say, What do you mean? It's private to her.

I've wanted to talk to her so often and now I can't think of anything to say. I just keep thinking, this is so expensive, this call is going so far, we'd better say something important. LONG DISTANCE is walking around in my brain.

"Katie?"

"Yeah?"

"Pay attention now, I don't have much time. I'll write, and then Dad can send me directions for how to get there."

"Okay."

"I'm pregnant."

The air in me falls out. I hold the phone tighter. I don't know what to say. Now she's really going to be in trouble. *Pregnant.* The word sounds like the thing it is. I am thinking, for some reason, of one grape, held in the air between somebody's two fingers.

"Are you there?" she asks. She's laughing a little.

"Yes, I'm here."
"I'm pregnant, I said. I'm married, too."
"Oh."
"But... don't tell Dad yet, okay?"
Well, I don't know.
"Don't tell him. I want to do it."
"All right."
"Just say I'll be coming."
"Yes."
"We'll be there the Wednesday before Thanksgiving. We'll make some pies. I miss you, Katie."
"Me, too."
When we hang up, I have an odd feeling that I made the whole thing up. But the receiver is warm. I have been on the phone. At my feet, my dog Bridgette is sitting and looking up at me. When I look down at her, she wags her tail. She wants out. I feel frozen. But Bridgette is squirming alive. I find her leash and put it on her. All she needs is to hear that little snapping sound and she turns around in circles like she's dancing a polka.
When I get outside, I look across the street and see the living-room blinds move. I don't think it's the parents, I don't think they'd be interested in watching. It's the kids. They're fourteen, and they're twins, Greg and Marsha. I believe they are relatives of the devil. I have never met anyone so deliberately mean for no reason. I didn't do anything but move here. I met them when we first came, like you have to, I have never asked them for anything, and they hate me. They leave notes in the bush out-

side my bedroom window. It started out with things like "Why don't you go back to Texas, cowgirl?" but now they have graduated to every swearword they know. I haven't told anyone. What good would it do? They wouldn't say, Oh, sorry, want to hang around with us now? The worst thing is, I read those notes, every time. I know what's going to be in them, but every time I open them and read them. I think about the hand, writing those notes, wearing a ring that it picked out. The notes are always in print, like script would be too nice.

I look away from the blinds, then back again, straight at them. I feel some strength just because Diane is coming. If they mess with her, she'll wind them around the telephone pole, tie them there with their arms. Plus I can tell Diane what they've done. Her, I can tell. I told Cherylanne, but I haven't heard back from her in a long time. I don't think she's exactly forgotten me, but if you said "Katie" to her she'd probably say, "Excuse me?"

I start walking Bridgette, figure in my head how long till Thanksgiving. Not long. Nineteen days. Not even one month. When I get home, I'll make a countdown sheet. And maybe my father will be up and I'll say, Guess what? He'll be glad, too, though he probably won't show it. He'll hold it back, it will only be in his face in a kind of stiffness. But he'll be glad. And I'll tell Ginger. All of a sudden, I have plans again. I'll write Cherylanne about how Diane was, all about how she looked and acted—Cherylanne always was interested in Diane because Diane paid no attention to her. I'll bet Diane is still so pretty, but with a pregnant stomach. I hope she's being careful. I think the skin over the baby is the really thin type. I think these blue lines run through it, that feed the baby. I don't see how, though. There's so much I need to find out now. I can have a project, keep some notes in a folder to show her when she gets here. A yellow one, for cheerfulness. I may find out things Diane never knew and she will be grateful. She may ask to keep the folder and I will let her. I'm going to be an aunt. Aunt Katie, I say to myself, but then I have to change it to Aunt Katherine. Which I like. I may put my hair in a bun when I'm around that baby. Plus I have some pearl clip-ons that from far away look exactly like pierced.

When I come in, my father is up, standing at the stove with his arms crossed, watching the coffee perk. He can't go by the smell, like my mother did. He has to watch the color. He has his blue plaid robe on, and his feet are bare. This is his morning outfit. He sleeps in a T-shirt and his boxer underpants and then he puts on his robe to come out and make coffee. You can see his Adam's apple, and how white and hairy his legs are. He kind of looks sad and too open, like a plucked chicken.

"She go?" he asks me, meaning the dog.

"Yup."

"All right."

He sits at the table, opens the paper.

"Did you hear the phone ring this morning?" I ask.

"No." He doesn't look up. He will in a minute.

"It was Diane. She's coming to visit."

Bingo. He looks up and closes the paper.

"When?"

"Thanksgiving."

"Where is she?"

"Still in Mexico. Dickie's coming, too."

His face still, thinking. He looks away from me, nods. Then he looks back down at the paper. His tongue is doing something inside his mouth.

"Are you glad?"

"Yeah. I'm glad." Still with the paper.

"I need to go to the grocery store. I'm making us Italian spaghetti tonight."

"All right."

I cross my legs, swing my foot, watch him reading. "I don't really like it here so far," I say.

"We haven't been here that long."

"Yes, but I still don't. Other places were much friendlier. The people here, they aren't friendly. The kids."

He goes over to the coffeepot, checks the color, turns off the flame, fills his cup. He takes a sip, looks over at me. "Wait awhile before you decide," he says. "See how you feel after a few months."

In my mind, there is a huge white calendar, big black numbers. You'd need a crane to lift the page.

I hear a thunking sound at my feet. Bridgette's bone. And then she lies beside it, sighs happy out her nose. There are ways of not needing much. I pet her by the curly hair at the back of her neck. She's a little like a cocker, with a lot of mystery thrown in. "Good girl," I say. "You're good. You just like your bone, don't you? Yes, you just like that bone."

"Katie," my father says.

I look up. "Yes?"

Nothing. Oh. He just means, Quiet, I'm trying to read. "You're a good girl," I tell Bridgette, whispering. "Yes, you are."

The next Wednesday, after school, I find a letter on my desk.

Dear Katie,
Well, I for one cannot believe how long it is since I wrote you. And you have written nineteen times! But if you knew what I've been doing you would be surprised I'm even writing now.

Number one is I am going steady with Todd Anderson and I don't *think I have to tell you he is a senior!! I have his ring on a chain, which I of course wear every day. It's getting serious and there are some questions I need to answer in my own mind if you know what I mean. Last slumber party when we played Truth or Dare someone asked me would I ever let him go to third base. I had to think a long time because we were playing for real. But I am happy to say I searched my heart and could honestly answer no, I would not. But you'll see when you go steady (anyway, DO you have a BOYFRIEND yet????) things get very serious in a fast way. I am going out with him tonight and I just finished my shower. I am under my hair dryer and it is so hot my ears are about to burn off! But of course you have to. I got a new shadow today, English Teaberry, which I recommend to you.*

I just read again in your one letter about those kids that put notes in your bushes. They are just backward and that's all. You should put notes in their bushes. See how they like it. Or you could tell their parents, which is more mature. That's what I would do. I would make an anonymous call and say, This is someone who cares, do you know what kind of children you have?

Listen to this. Bubba is quarterback now on the football team. He is so big he can hardly fit in king-size britches. He gets away with everything on account of practice is so hard, *boo-hoo. He gets the most food as usual but now he gets it in between times too, the best things get saved for King Bubba and pity you if you eat it. He gets to sleep late every weekend and I as usual do all the work around here.*

You asked if I look the same. Well, not really. I have longer hair and I wear it in a flip with a headband that matches what I wear. Which of course is all different from when you were here. A lot of people say I look like that model that is all the time in Seventeen *magazine (if you don't read it, get it NOW it is SO GOOD and has so many quizzes and helpful hints) and I don't think it is bragging on myself to say I do agree. If you look in this month's issue, there she is on page 31 with that plaid pleated skirt and mohair sweater. Hers is black but I got white. It shows off jewelry better. And of course you have to be a little careful with black, what people might think you are saying! Anyway, if you look at that picture of that model, it's like seeing me, everyone says so.*

I liked your school picture, but Katie you need to remember to comb your hair before they take it. Just carry a fold-up rattail, they have them in tor-

toiseshell and white, and just keep it in your purse and it is always on the ready. It makes a difference. Not that I mean to be critical. You would know if you could hear me say it, that I am being kind. In writing it looks critical but it's really not.

Well, thank God my hair is finally *dry! I have to finish getting ready. I am up to my favorite part of putting perfume on my pulse points. You remember you have to do that half an hour before they arrive or you smell too much and it is vulgar. It is Saturday night, the big one.*

I hope everything is okay there. Well I mean I hope it gets better. I know it will!! Sometimes you have to try to be friendlier, you've always been so quiet. Try this. Next time you go to school, smile in the halls. Just smile! One thing people cannot resist is a friendly smile and a flirty wave of the hand. The boys. And the girls like a smile themselves. Good-bye for now,

Love,

Cherylanne

I put the letter in my underwear drawer. Cherylanne's pile is pitiful low. Two letters and one postcard. I go out into the kitchen, where Ginger is cleaning the sink. "You know that envelope you put on my desk?" I say.

She turns around, and the rag she is holding drips two pure drops onto the floor. "Yes?" she says, and then, noticing the drips, turns quickly back to the sink, throws the rag in there. Then she wipes her hands on her apron. She has on a green shift under that, with some geometry shapes on it. Plus her hair is fixed up, bouffant style with some curls over her cheeks. She must have a date tonight. Sometimes she'll go right from work. Her boyfriend's name is Wayne, but I can tell she doesn't think that much of him. She is never excited when they're going out. It's more of a second-prize feeling.

"That was a long letter from my best friend in Texas. Cherylanne."

"Oh. That's a nice name. Cherylanne. I like that."

"Well," I say, casual so she'll know it's true, "She was very popular. She still is."

"Nice to have a friend like that."

"Yes." I look over the fruit bowl, select an apple. "But now I have friends here."

Ginger smiles. "I'm glad. When do I get to meet some of them?"

"Well, so far it's really only one. But more are on the way."

"Who is the one?"

"Her name is Cynthia O'Connell. I can ride my bike to her house. Which I am going to do now. But I'll bring her here next time, if you want."

"That would be nice. I'd like to meet her."

I go back to my room, sit on my bed. Well, it's official, now. I have kind of broken up with Cherylanne, telling Ginger about my new friend. I would have always had Cherylanne first, but she just couldn't write back. I wasn't her real friend, anyway. She was too old.

Now I have found a friend my own age. I have to admit that I don't like her as much as Cherylanne. At least not yet. She's different. Not as interesting or kind of lit-up, like Cherylanne was. But maybe that's good, and as I get to know her better I will collect things about her, and she will become the one I tell things to. I squeeze out some tears for Cherylanne and then I go to get my bike.

Outside, Greg is on his lawn, throwing a football to some friend of his. Marsha is sitting on the steps, eating marshmallows out of the bag. Something she doesn't know about me is that is one of my favorite things, too. You can toast them over the stove on a fork, you don't need a campfire. I don't think either of them will say anything with Greg's friend there. But I am wrong. "Hey, dipshit!" Greg yells.

"Greg!" Marsha says. What she means is, "Yeah, get her, let's have some more fun." But I guess she has a crush on the friend so she is acting like oh my delicate self is so offended by this tough talk.

I don't say anything. Last time they made fun of the dog. I wished so hard she would attack them but all she did was wag her tail and strain at the leash for them to pet her. I tried to send thoughts down into her but no, she liked them.

I walk my bike down the driveway and don't look over. "Hey!" Greg says. "It's November! You don't ride your bike in November!"

Well, I do. *I* do, pecker head. I can feel my

brain wishing my mouth would rear up and speak those very words back to him. But I can't do it.

"She's so weird," Greg tells his friend. Loudly.

"What's your problem, Greg?" the friend asks. He is halfway between puzzled and laughing. I see he is holding the football at his hip like they do. It's kind of like their purse.

"She's the new neighbor," Greg says, and it sounds like he's taking some bad food out of his mouth.

"So?" I hear the friend ask as I am riding away. He seems like an angel to me. Compared to Greg. I saw that he had blond hair. I pump hard, wish so much that I had a three speed. I'll ask for one for Christmas. "Something wrong with your old bike?" he'll ask. And I'll say no, nothing is wrong with it.

One thing I already know about Cynthia is that she has a Princess phone. In her own bedroom. It's pink, and if you use it at night when the lights are out, no problem, it has a light-up dial right in the receiver. I guess you have to quick put your ear there after you dial or the person you are calling will just be hanging in space saying, Hello? Hello?

Another thing I know is she is an only child and her closet has two doors on it. That is more or less as far as we've gotten from talking at lunch. What she knows about me is I'm an army brat from Texas.

I find her house pretty easily, it's just like she told me how to get there. It's a big house, too, also like she told me, and she has a weeping willow in her front yard so she is even luckier. I turn into her driveway, then lay my bike down on the front lawn. I ring her doorbell, which is the rich-people chime, and her mother opens it.

"Katie?" she says, smiling.

"Yes, ma'am." The mother is very pretty, curly brown hair with a scarf tied in it. A pants and sweater outfit, gray, with some pearl buttons and even gray shoes. Her cheeks are rosy pink and she has light blue eyes. Cynthia's eyes are like that, but I am sorry to say I don't think she's as pretty as her mother. Cynthia already has a little bit of a complexion problem which we haven't talked about yet since it's so recent that we decided to become friends. Later, I can tell her some things I know about complexions. Like you wash your face with boiling hot water and rinse with freezing cold. This shocks your pores and then they behave. Once Cherylanne started crying after she did a face treatment and I said well then why do you do it so hot? and she said the more severe you do it the better you look. She said you know how they always say you have to suffer for your beauty, well how do you think that got started?

I start to go into Cynthia's house, but Mrs. O'Connell puts her hand to my shoulder, light. "Is that your bike, dear?" she asks.

I look back, as though the bike might have changed into someone else's. Now already I have done a dumb thing.

"Yes, ma'am."

"Well," she says, and looks troubled, little puffs of flesh come between her eyebrows. And then she says, "Let's you and I go out together and we'll move it, how's that?"

"Okay." I follow her back out.

She picks up my bike and wheels it over to the side of the garage, props it there. "Now, you see, it's out of the way," she says. And I nod. One thing I know is my mother would never have done a thing like this. She tried hard to be polite to the other person's way of looking at things. Plus she knew what was worth it to say and what wasn't. This was definitely not worth it. I feel like leaving, but there is Cynthia, waving from the front porch. Well, she of course is the one I came to see.

"Cynthia!" Mrs. O'Connell yells to her. "In in in! It's too cold for you to be out here!"

Cynthia disappears back inside and I meet up with her again in the hallway. She takes my coat for me, formal as you please, and then we go upstairs. One thing I see is they have wall-to-wall carpeting. The steps feel like they are higher than they are.

Cynthia has a canopy bed, white and pink, and a fuzzy pink rug on the floor beside it, which makes for two rugs because of the wall-to-wall. Wide pink ribbons tie her ruffly curtains back. They look like party girls bowing to each other. I see her Princess phone on the table beside the bed on its own doily. Later, I'll ask to use it.

Cynthia sits down on her bed and puts her hands in her lap, jiggles her leg a little. "Did you find the house okay?" she asks. Inside myself I'm saying, Whew, this girl is worse off than me. I don't think she's hardly ever had a kid come over to see her.

"Yeah, it was easy," I say. "It was just like you drew."

I am still standing there. I'm not sure that I can really sit on the bed beside Cynthia and I don't want to sit on the floor. There's a flowered chair by the window, but it's full of fancy pillows.

We look at each other a little, and then I figure I might as well take the plunge. "Does your phone really work?" I ask, sitting down beside her.

She nods.

"Could I try it?"

"Well..." She moves her head in a way that looks like it's trying to slide off her neck. And then, "Okay."

"I'll just do operator."

I pick up the phone and I have to say they're right, it is a little exciting, all the light-up numbers right there in the receiver. It makes for a coziness in the stomach. I dial 0, and when the operator comes on, I hang up. "It works, all right," I say.

"You can talk on it if you want."

"That's okay."

Cynthia's door opens and her mother pokes her head in. "Honey?" she says. "Do you *need* this door closed?"

Well, I'm the one who did it. It's an automatic thing to me, that when two friends go into one of them's bedroom, you close the door. Then you have made your own place. You can talk.

"I did it," I say.

"You closed the door?"

"Yes, ma'am."

"Uh-huh. Well, that's all right. You didn't know. We'll just leave it open now, though, would that be all right?"

"Sure." Like I am really the one deciding.

"Did you girls want a snack?"

Cynthia looks at me.

"I don't care," I say. "Either way." I don't want one because the mother has ruined my mood.

"Yes, please," Cynthia says.

"Be right back," her mother says, her voice trying to make up, sounding as soothing as the school nurse when she takes out the thermometer and sees that you really are sick. I can just imagine what the snack will be. Pea soup or something like that. Cucumber sandwiches, or mixed nuts in a fancy bowl. Or watercress, which I don't even know what is. Nothing like just a bag of bar-b-que chips and a couple of Dr Peppers.

"Mariannnnnnna!!" I hear coming from somewhere nearby. It's an old lady's voice, thin and shaky, but full of rage.

"Just one moment, Mother," Mrs. O'Connell calls back.

"No, NOOOOOWWWWW!!" the woman yells.

Mrs. O'Connell smiles at us. Lipstick is clear to the exact corners of her mouth. "I'll be back with your snack in a little while," she says.

Next I hear her low tone talking from somewhere down the hall and the old woman yelling back in another language. I look at Cynthia.

"That's my grandmother." She shrugs. "She's Italian."

"Oh." I never have gotten to have grandparents. One thing my parents had in common when they met is that their parents were dead. It was kind of an odd connection, but they took it as step one.

"Do you want to play the Barbie Game?" Cynthia asks.

No. But what can you do on the first time? I say all right, and Cynthia opens her grand-size closet to take the game down from the shelf. I see a blue velvet dress in there that goes all the way to the floor. It has plastic wrapping over it. "Is that yours?" I ask.

"Yes. It's for piano recitals." She is kneeling on the floor, setting the game up. "Who do you want to be?"

"Barbie."

"Ohhhhhhh!" she says, disappointed like her cat has been killed.

"Well, I don't care," I say. "I'll be Midge."

Now she is happy again. I really miss Cherylanne.

When we are playing, her mother comes in with a tray. She sets it down beside us. On it is cheese and crackers. Well, it could have been worse. The drink is orange juice in glasses with polka dots on them. "Mariannnna!" we all hear again. Mrs. O'Connell smiles a smile that is a sigh, and walks out of the room, her back straight as a fence post.

I roll the die, take my turn. Then I check the sky, see if it's turning dark yet.

We play in silence for a while, and then Cynthia says, "I can vag fart."

I look up. "Pardon me?"

"I can vag fart."

I don't say anything.

"Fart from my vagina."

"What do you mean?"

Cynthia stands, moves to a corner of her bedroom, lies on the floor, raises her legs up against her chest and makes an odd sound come out of her. Well, what is a person supposed to do. "Uh-huh," I say. And then, "Well, I have to get going."

"It's *early*!" Cynthia says, sitting up.

"I know, but I have an appointment. With the dentist."

"We're not done playing! We need dates and you still need a dress!"

"I know. But we can just say you won. You would have won."

Cynthia frowns, begins putting the game away. I start to help her and she says, "No, I'll do it. You have to *go,* remember?"

"Well, I have a couple of minutes."

She says nothing, continues stacking up the cards. I see the careful part in her hair and I all of a sudden feel sorry for her. She can't help it that she's so strange. She doesn't know how to do friends. And anyway, she's all I have.

"So... you play piano?" I ask.

She keeps her head down, nods.

"Will you show me next time?"

She looks up, hope. "Yeah! I'll teach you 'By the Sea,' you can learn that in one second."

Well now, that would be worth it. I have always wanted to learn to play a piano. "By the Sea," I think, and see the gulls spinning their slow circles over noisy waves. I have an idea already how the song might go: a rush of notes up, and then a tired coming down.

"Want to meet my grandmother before you go?" Cynthia asks.

"That's okay."

"She's funny. You'll like her. She's only mean to my mother. She really likes kids."

Well, when you are on your way out you can do more things than you might ordinarily. "All right," I say.

Cynthia leads me to a room at the end of the hall. Here, the door is closed. Cynthia knocks quietly, then pushes the door open. In a bed by the window, I see a very small old lady propped up on pillows. Her hair is thin and bright white and wild about her head. She has huge brown eyes, focused on us like magnets to metal. She is wearing a brown plaid flannel shirt open over a pale blue nightgown, and she has one of those knobby chests, mystery bones sticking out all over the place. She has many rings on her fingers. I see a square blue stone, a round yellow one, some diamonds.

"What's-a matta?" she yells. "Who's-a this?"

"It's my friend Katie," Cynthia says.

"Come over here," the old lady says, quieter, and I step a little closer.

She slams her hand down on the bed, mutters something at the ceiling in Italian. Then she looks at me and says, "*Here,* scaredy girl! Little wa-wa! Come here so I can-a see you!"

I move closer and she sits up, leans forward,

cranes her skinny neck out like a mean bird. She stares at my shoes, and then her gaze travels slowly all the way up to my face. Then, as though exhausted, she leans back against her pillows, closes her eyes. "She's-a nice," she says, nearly in a whisper. "It's okay."

"In school, we have history together," Cynthia says.

Her grandmother nods, then opens her eyes wide. "What's-a the clock?"

"Four-fifteen," Cynthia tells her.

"Put him on! Put him on!" the grandmother says, and Cynthia moves to a television positioned on a nearby dresser so that it can be seen from the bed. She turns the knob and a soap opera comes on. You can spot them a mile away. All the people with the same kind of face, kind of secret and like they're playing a joke on themselves. Like when the director says "Cut!" they'll all explode laughing. Cherylanne used to like soap operas. Once she dreamed what was going to happen the next day and it did. She was hard to live with for awhile because she thought that was such a big deal. She said, "This dream has told me that I could be a writer. That is now one of my career options."

The soap opera Cynthia has turned on is a famous one that takes place in a hospital, I forget the name. The old lady holds out a trembling finger, points to the screen, at the doctor and nurse who are standing beside each other in a patient's room. The patient has about nine hundred bandages on. The doctor is talking to him and the nurse is watching the doctor.

"Ha!" The grandmother says. "You see her, that nurse, she's-a stand by the doctor?"

"Yes," I say.

"She's-a *fuck* him."

"Nona!" Cynthia says, and then starts laughing. And so do I.

"Yes! That sullamabeech, he's-a sleep with everybody! And one woman, Susan, he's-a marry her *twice*! *Che puzza!*"

"What's that mean?" I ask Cynthia quietly.

" 'Disgusting,' " Cynthia says. "Once she got mad and threw her shoe at the TV. It broke the screen."

Well, this visit has picked up. I'll come back here.

Nona pulls a bag of hard candy from the drawer in her bedside table, pops a piece into her mouth. Without taking her eyes from the screen, she offers the bag to us. Even from where I am, I can still see the lint all over the colored balls. "No, thank you," I say.

"She has a dentist appointment," Cynthia says.

"Sssshhhh!" Nona waves her hand at us. We are dismissed.

On the way downstairs, Cynthia says, "She's always like that. You can't control her. She fights with my mother all the time. It's kind of embarrassing."

Zipping up my coat at the door, I say, "I like her."

"Oh. Good," Cynthia says, and relief is there, soft as a leaf that falls at your feet.

"Are you *leaving* already?" I hear from the kitchen, and Cynthia's mother appears. She is wearing an apron with a built-in towel, and holding a potato peeler. Cynthia and I have already made up about my going. I don't know why her mother has to butt in.

"I have a dentist appointment," I say. I am sort of starting to believe it. I have a smell in my nose of dentists' hands. "Thank you for having me."

"Well, you're *wel*come," Mrs. O'Connell says, and I can tell from her tone she knows I'm lying. I can feel her watching me as I go to get my bike. She is a sticky kind of person, like a spider in a web. I'll tell Cynthia to come to my house next time.

When I get home, my father is there, standing in the entryway. "Where were you?" he asks. His eyes are flat angry. There is a white crumb of something he was eating on his cheek and I am careful not to look at it.

"I was at Cynthia O'Connell's house. I told Ginger."

"Uh-huh. Well, you didn't tell me. Did you?"

"You weren't here. So I just told Ginger."

"She has nothing to do with this. When you want to do something, you ask me, not her. In case you have forgotten, I am your father. I decide where you will and will not go."

I am not ready to take on the load of this. He has been so much better lately, I'd forgotten how he can turn. The thing to do is get past him, let it soak in that I am home now, he can be done.

"Sorry." I start to walk past him.

He puts his hand on my shoulder, pushes me back in front of him. "I'm telling you," he says. "Don't you start this. Don't you be taking off places without telling me."

Oh. I see. He's been thinking of Diane.

"Sorry," I say again, and this time he lets me go.

In my room, I take out Cherylanne's few letters, hold them all together, sort through them one by one, then hold them all together again. I can smell the dinner he's making. Liver and onions, which I hate so much. Sometimes he makes bacon with it too and then I can mostly cover it up. I put Cherylanne's letters back, start my homework, and don't look up until he calls me to eat.

"People, PEople!" Mr. Hadd says. "This is BABY work! *One* leads to *two* leads to *three!* What is the *prob*lem with this problem? What do you not understand?" He is so genuinely amazed. Like a star has landed in his lap. Big fat eyeballs, looking out at us. And wounded, too. He looks at us like we have broken his heart. "Katie," he says. "What do *you* not understand?"

"Well, just the part... I think..." I hate math so bad. I hate Mr. Hadd so bad. I take in a breath. "I don't understand one thing you just said. On account of I'm a dummy. *Duh.*" I hear from the little muffled and surprised sounds the class is making I am a hero.

"Is that right?" he says, but what he means is, keep it up and you'll go to pay your regards to the principal. That's what he calls it, pay your regards. Eduardo Hernandez pays his regards about once a week. He always leaves smirking, but when he comes back his face is a little caved in. Everyone is nice enough not to stare at him, but since he sits right across from me I can't help but see his hurt feelings. Well, now it might be my turn. Mr. Hadd is boring his eyeballs into me. I can keep on my path to make kids like me, or I can be quiet. I don't really want to go to the principal's office.

I think I could make a good case for myself, but also they might tell my father. I shrug, look down at my desk, let the teacher win. I have other things to do besides get in trouble in math class.

Mr. Hadd sighs and turns to the blackboard, starts writing. He is about squeezing that chalk to death. I watch him put numbers and symbols down, but I am thinking about a new girl I met in our English class today. Taylor Sinn is her name. Sinn! She got seated in front of me. She had a big black purse like grown women have, the good kind of leather. It was gaping open and I saw a pack of cigarettes in there. Benson & Hedges, menthol. Also a spray bottle of perfume and a natural-bristle brush that is not in drugstores, you have to get them in department stores. She's really tall, but she's still our age. She has green eyes slanted just a little to be so interesting, and she has long thick blond hair, straight as a board, and she wears a thin black velvet ribbon to hold it back. Kind of like Alice in Wonderland. I never saw hair like that, shot through with a kind of sparkle. I had to rein myself in not to touch it. I have tried ironing my hair but it has never been so straight as that.

Taylor looked like a model, really pretty, with a face like someone drew it and stood back and said, "Now *there!*" Her clothes were all just perfect, a heather-colored A-line skirt, a Peter-Pan collar shirt and a heather cardigan. Circle pin. And Weejuns, burgundy. The boys were all having heart attacks and the girls got bristly and moved their butts around in their chairs and tried to act like they didn't notice her when meanwhile they were practically breaking their necks turning around in little ways to have a look. Taylor knew the answers to every question Mrs. Brady asked, but about halfway through class she got bored and stopped raising her hand. I saw her elbow move from doodling and once I saw part of what she was doing, which was writing words in big fat letters, the kind that are sort of like clouds and lean into each other. I know how to do that, too. She came from a private school, the Bartlett School for Girls. It's on a hill, really fancy, with a big sign in front and lacy gates, buildings with ivy growing up them. We drive past it a lot and I always wonder what it would be like to go there. I don't know why anyone would leave a place like that to come here, where half the water fountains don't work. But the cigarettes might be why. She might be the reckless type, which interests me quite a bit.

"Katie?" Mr. Hadd says. "Want to let the rest of us in on the daydream?"

I look up, try to think fast. And then the bell rings. I don't get up right away, out of respect for the fact that Mr. Hadd was about to yell at me. But he clucks his tongue and shakes his head, then looks away. I can go. He will stare out the window and think, what oh what can I, Harry Hadd, do with these lamebrains?

Out in the hall, Eduardo taps me on the shoulder. "Saved by the bell," he says. "Get it?"

"Yes," I say. And we smile. It is friendly. I see that Eduardo has a bit of gold on one of his teeth. Now we know a little about each other. This is my best day so far.

Two days away from when Diane is to come, the weather turns serious cold. Everything gets frozen, including the pond a few blocks away. It's a small thing, hidden behind a Mobil gas station. I like it because it's so private. In the summer, I could wade to the middle and the water would still be below my knees. I will be able to ice-skate there now, and one thing I like is to ice-skate, although I am plain terrible at it. You would think after awhile a person could at least just skate straight ahead. I think I have bad ankles, though, because they lean in toward each other. I can't stand straight on ice skates. I wobble and fall a lot. Still, this does not keep me from the main pleasure of it, which is that when I skate, in my head I see ballerinas. I have seen them on television often, and once my mother took me to see them for real. I was young, only six, but I remember every single detail about that day, including that sitting in front of me was a woman wearing one of those stoles where the foxes bite each other's tails, and black round beads are where their eyes used to be. I still do not understand this idea. It seems like whoever made it up was saying, Ho, let's see just how much I can get away with. The sight of that stole made me feel sick in the knees but I just looked around it to watch the ballerinas. I stayed so still watching them I had a crick in my neck later. They were so, so beautiful and of another world. That's how it seemed to me. Their faces were full of a glowing peace and their movements were so smooth and silky, like I had no idea a real person could be. Their legs were very long, and their necks. It seemed like their fingers trailed behind their fingers. They had their hair up in plain but beautiful buns like Grace Kelly. One of them wore a little diamond crown, and when the light caught it right the sparkle would shine out so hard and far it made you feel like blinking. They wore white see-through skirts with wide ribbon ties that hung down and fluttered in the back. My mother used to tell me when I was little to go to sleep so the fairies could come and paint stars on my ceiling. She said they wouldn't come unless I was asleep. This of course posed a dilemma. But anyway, I had imagined those fairies wearing dresses just like the ballerinas, so it was kind of a shock pleasure to see them for real. Now I think it would be a shock to see ballerinas dressed in anything but those dresses or doing things like walking around flat. I hope I never do see that.

Anyway, that is why I like to skate. I don't like to bring anyone else with me to puncture the dream.

After school, I find my ice skates and head for the pond. I have worn my watch to keep track of the time. Our arrangement is that I can go places if I tell Ginger exactly where, and get home before he does. He acted like I was getting a big raise in allowance, two million a week. And I acted low grateful.

Nobody is on the street. It's too cold. Being out here makes my cheeks hurt and my eyes water; the air I breathe in makes the back of my throat feel raw. Yet I like it, too. It's kind of exciting. It's like the air is saying, "HERE!" and your body is saying, "YES, I CAN DO IT!!"

The pond is frozen, all right, and ringed by weeds that have been frosted stiff white. I sit down, pull off my boots, and the air gets in right through two layers of socks. You have to respect that. I put on my skates, line my boots up, then walk crookedly over to the ice. I test the edge with one foot. It's frozen solid. I walk out a few steps, stand still to take in some breaths of preparation air. And then I start gliding. It's going well; the ice is not too bumpy and I can go pretty fast. I take a turn around the outside edges and don't fall once. Then I do it again. Then, since I apparently have all of a sudden mastered that, I think maybe I'll try something harder. I stop, try to skate backward, and fall down. Well, there. I knew it. It's always a surprise the first time you fall. That's the one that hurts the most. Usually by the time I'm done skating falling is so natural I don't feel it at all. I get up quickly now, try again. But nothing happens except that I take wobbly baby steps in the backward direction. Plus I am ugly bent over like a person mopping a floor. This is the opposite of what to do to think about ballerinas.

I try pushing off hard to go faster, and fall again. Falling can actually be boring.

In the center of the pond, the ice looks smoother. I'll try there. At real rinks, the center is where the really good skaters always leap and spin. And they seem not to be thinking about it at all, not even really trying. Maybe that's the secret, you have to be nonchalant, let the actions sneak up on your brain without telling it what you're going to do. I think you stick one leg out, pull it in, and violà, you're spinning like a top. I go out to the center and try this, think deliberately about nothing, and then quick stick my leg out. It doesn't work. I fall hard this time, crack the back of my head against the ice. I lie there for a while, stunned, looking at the blue sky above me. Then, as I am getting up onto my knees, I fall through the ice. The water is so cold that at first I don't feel it. But then I do, and it hurts so bad. I am on my hands and knees in the middle of the pond like a wrong kind of dog. I see my boots over on the shore and they look so warm and friendly to me. If only I can live I can put them on again. I stand up, crash through some more ice, then find some that will hold me. I skate back to the edge of the pond, walk over and sit down by my boots. My teeth are chattering so hard I think I might bite my tongue and start bleeding down my chest. But I don't. I try to unlace my skates, but I can't. They are too wet and my fingers won't work anyway. I squeeze one hand with the other and water runs out of my mitten. And now I can't separate the fingers I've squeezed together. Fear comes into me. I wonder should I yell *help,* but I feel too stupid. I try anyway. I say, "Help," in a normal voice. And then I start crying. The tears feel hot.

I look around, see the Mobil station. I'll go in there, ask if I can use the ladies' room, and warm up. I'll get warm enough to go home. And then I'll never come here again.

It takes so long to get to the station. It is hard to walk on skates, that is not exactly what the designer had in mind. By the time I get there, I feel cold all the way to the core of me. A bell tinkles when I open the door, not the Christmas kind, just a regular kind to say to the attendant, Look alive, a customer's here. I see a man seated at a desk in the corner. He is reading a newspaper, and he doesn't look up. He reads like me, I think, and then I can't believe it, but I fall down.

"Excuse me," I say.

The man looks up, then rushes over to me. I am an emergency. "Oh, my God," he says. "What happened here?"

"I was skating," I say, and then stop talking. I'm shivering too much to talk right now. The floor feels so warm against me. It is a dark linoleum with some yellow specks in it. I see a little puddle starting to form around me and I try to push the water back under me. "I'm l-l-leaking," I say.

"Wait right here," the man says, and goes into a back room. When he comes out, he is holding an outfit like mechanics wear. It's a faded blue color. "Jimmy" is sewn in red in fancy embroidery over on one side.

"Take this back there and change into it."

I look at him.

"You need to get out of those wet clothes."

I'm not sure what to do.

"Really!" he says.

I just keep looking at him. I notice that my teeth are still chattering. They are making a loud, clicking sound. I think this is how people with false teeth sound when they eat.

The man sighs, worried impatient, and then bends down to take my skates off. It's hard for him, too, but he does it. And then I get up, walk back where he told me to go. My feet make squishy sounds, leave big marks. I can't really feel them.

I feel so embarrassed taking my clothes off, but the door is locked and anyway, I've started to think I might die if I don't change. My underwear is still dry, thank goodness, and I leave that on. Otherwise I would have that dilemma of where do I put my bra.

I come back out into the room and the man looks at my bare feet. "Oh," he says, and sits down, starts taking his shoes off.

"That's okay," I say, and so does he! Right exactly after I say it, he says it too.

He hands me his socks and then he puts his shoes back on without them.

"I don't want to take your socks," I say.

"Put them on," he says, and I do. They do not have a smell, which is so courteous.

He's mopped up all the water while I changed, and the place feels luxurious now, all dry and closed against the wind. He sits down and laces his fingers across his stomach, leans back in his chair, looks at me. Now that we are done with the drama part, we can relax a little. "So what happened?" he asks. "Did you fall through?"

"Yes," I say, and then, "it was very solid at the edges."

"Yeah, you can't really tell." He covers up for my ignorance just like me.

A bell rings from outside, loud. A car is there, pulled up to the pump. The white smoke that pours from the tailpipe is all hysterical looking, like smoke gets in real cold weather. Just ripping out of that pipe like escaped snakes, then flat disappearing. "Be right back," the man says. He goes out and talks to the driver, then puts the nozzle in the gas hole. He pops open the hood, checks the oil. He cleans the windshield perfectly. He does this all without even trying. Then he hangs up the nozzle, takes the driver's money, says something to him, and comes back in fast, stamping his feet to get the warmth back.

"Whoa!" he says. "Cold!" And then, "Would you like some hot chocolate?"

I nod. The Queen of England has never felt better than this. It is something to be saved. And this man is shiver-handsome. He really is. He has brown wavy hair and blue eyes like Superman. He is wearing jeans and a red-checked flannel shirt, and the buttons are open at the top of his throat in a way I can't look at. Although I did see a *V* of very white T-shirt and some dark curly hairs reaching up. He puts some coins from his own pocket in a machine in the corner of the room, then hands me a thick paper cup. It is the too-dark, skinny kind of cocoa but I know that now it will taste delicious to me. Say I could even have marshmallows. "No thanks," I would say. "Don't need them."

"Where do you live?" the man asks. "Can I call your folks for you?"

Even after all this time, I still get a hard knot of pain when I have to tell people that my mother is dead. "I only have a father," I say. That's how I do it. I keep her out of it, for sacred reasons.

"Oh. So... should I call him?"

"No!" I say quickly. Oh, boy. My father would have what they call a field day with this. "You *what?*" he would say about nine thousand times. And then of course I'd get punished. No. I don't think I'll tell him. I'll just let my clothes dry and then go home. The man has draped my things out on the desk top. But they are awfully wet. They're going to take a long time to get dry. I look at my watch. It's wrecked. "Do you have the time?"

He looks at *his* watch. "Four-twenty."

I'll never make it.

But then I think of something. "Would you mind if I borrowed this uniform? Could I just wear it home and give it back tomorrow?"

"Sure."

This is working out fine. I can get back and dry everything before he gets home. Ginger won't say anything to him, I know she won't. I can trust her.

"Are you Jimmy?" I ask.

He nods, smiles. "Well, actually, Jim."

"Oh. I'm Katie. I'm sorry I fell in."

"Don't be sorry, I'm just glad you're all right. I watched you skating for a little while. And then I got involved with the newspaper. Sports page." He adds that part low, like he's a little embarrassed.

"I like the sports page," I say, even though this is not so true.

"You're a good skater."

I look down. "No, I'm not."

"Well, you're beginning, I know. But you have a very graceful way about you."

"No, I don't."

"You do! And listen, I know a lot about skating."

"You do?"

"Well, hockey. I know about hockey. Played it in high school." He looks out the window at the pond. "Huh. Years ago, now."

"How old are you?" I ask. Disaster can make a person bold.

"I'm twenty-three. How about you?"

"Fifteen," I say.

He looks more closely at me.

"Well, in a few weeks I will be." It is true that in a few weeks I'll be thirteen. My birthday is in December, the gyp month for birthdays.

He smiles. "I see."

His teeth are white like a toothpaste commercial. Whew! my insides are saying.

"Well," I say. "I'd better go."

"I don't think you should walk home. You're still awful cold, aren't you?"

I had forgotten, but yes, I am.

"How far away is your house?"

"Just two blocks. I can make it."

"I'll give you a ride," he says, standing up.

"You can't do that."

"Sure, I can."

"Somebody might come."

"They can wait."

"Won't you get in trouble with your boss?"

"I'm the manager," he says, just as plain as could be, not bragging one bit. He gathers up my things, throws a bunch of keys up in the air and catches them. You can tell athletic people just from how they do things like that. I'll bet he was captain of the hockey team at least. I think of him being in high school, and it makes my stomach jump a little. Him walking down the hall, books at his hip, sweater sleeves pushed up. Every girl in the school just wishing.

"Let's go," he says, and I go outside, which feels so much warmer to me now. He locks the door to the office, goes over to a big tow truck, opens the door for me. I am dying inside of a multitude of things. Like, how do I look climbing in? In front of this man who is so tall and handsome. And opening the door for me like we are going out to dine in a French restaurant. *Let's,* he'd said, as if we were a couple.

We talk some on the way home, but it's such a short ride we can't get too deep. Mostly it's directions. I sneak a few looks at him. He is really handsome, he is killer handsome. Like those men you see in magazines that you say oh sure I'd like to see someone who really looks like that. Well, here he is. When I get out, I say, "Thanks for everything. I'll bring this back tomorrow."

"I'll be there," he says, and this shocks me, that he has been there for a while, and that he will be there tomorrow, just like that.

Ginger tells me to take a warm bath, she'll dry my clothes. This is what I mean about her. Plus she made oatmeal raisin cookies and what I predict is that when I get out of the bathtub she will have three or four out on a little plate for me, with a glass of milk and a napkin folded triangle style. When I am done in the tub, I come out to the kitchen in my towel to check. Bingo. And she's off running the vacuum, not hovering nearby to hear how great she is. Or to say anything about the dumbness of people skating on thin ice.

I go into my room, change into pajamas. I'm done with clothes for today. I put Jimmy's uniform under my pillow. Later I will touch it to help me take out the memory of all that happened today. You need time for that kind of thing. The kind of time where you know you are not going to be interrupted, so that the shy thoughts will say, Oh well fine, I guess it's all right to come out now.

In home ec, we are making pudding. I have to admit that now I am interested. Because I didn't know you don't have to use the little boxes from the store, you can actually make your own from scratch. The magic ingredient is cornstarch. Miss Woods held up the yellow box and she kept pointing to it with her manicured finger like it was a prize being given away on TV. She said a little speech about all cornstarch could do, and it ended with you can even use it on a baby's butt to protect it from diaper rash. So I will write that in the notebook for Diane. I have six pages so far of things I've learned. Including that babies can hear inside there before they are born! I would bet one hundred dollars that Diane does not know that. I will need to show her the book where I found it, and even then she will stand there doubting, with her hand on her hip. I can hardly believe that tomorrow I will see her.

I am making chocolate pudding, but on the other stoves they're making butterscotch and vanilla. I like butterscotch best, but you have to take your assignment. I am doing the stirring part, which of course you do alone. My teammates are at one of the tables smashing graham crackers to make a piecrust and talking low enough that I can't hear them. Just a day or so ago this would have made me feel lonely but now I welcome the time to let my head think of my own things.

I stare at the gingham curtains Miss Woods has hanging at the windows. They are hung in what she calls the gay way. She says, "The cook's domain should say to all who enter, 'Welcome and be happy!' " She told us the trick that if you should ever live in a place where the kitchen doesn't have windows, why, no problem, just put the curtains on the wall and it will give you psychological pleasure. I stare at the curtains and remember again, in slow-motion detail, Jimmy taking my skates off. Jimmy standing up and saying, "Let's go." Last night I lay in bed with his uniform over me. It had a slight smell of oil and man, mixed together. It didn't smell bad, it smelled personal. I realized that in just those few minutes I had developed a full crush. But different this time. Before, when I knew that I was starting to love a boy, it was like a yip in my heart. Now that it's a man, it feels like a fan unfolding. Or like when they show the flowers on those science shows, where you can see them open. Like that. Or a shy woman coming into the room with just that one person, the door closed behind them, and she takes off her scarf and there is her hair, golden as could be, and she never even knew. The heart of myself has always been something just wanting so bad. I have had an empty center, black as a basement, but also knowing about light, and waiting. Young as I am, I know now that everything is about to come. Jimmy will be the place for me to learn the real happiness. He will be my Joy School. My joy. Mine.

"Katie," Miss Woods says in my ear. "You're burning the bottom." I startle, look into my saucepan. She is right. I scrape the bottom, and black flecks float up. This will not work so well for Heavenly Cloud Pie. "I'll help you fix it," Miss Woods says quietly. She is being nice because she thinks I'm just bad at pudding. She doesn't know I wasn't paying attention at all for awhile. And I am not about to set the record straight. I nod okay.

Miss Woods steps away from me, claps her hands to get everyone's attention. Sometimes she thinks she's teaching nursery school. "All right now, girls," she says. "We're getting to the most exciting part of all!" You would think we were on a safari and she is about to show us a live rhino. For Miss Woods, the high parts of something are very easy to get to. She is one of those types you know will always be happy and you can't help but feel jealous of them even while you look at them strangely.

When I get home, I see Jimmy's uniform on the kitchen table, washed and folded. It's Ginger's and my secret and she is holding up her end even more than she has to. I tell her thank you very much.

"It was no problem," she says. "I was doing a load anyway."

"Still," I say.

"I probably don't have to tell you this, Katie, but don't try skating today."

"Oh, I'm not. I'm just bringing the uniform back."

"Cynthia called, just before you came home. I told her you'd call her back."

Well, not now. This is one rule about mixing boys and girls, that a date always comes first. Cherylanne told me, "Any girl who is a true friend knows that she must support you in your pursuit of romance." The day she told me that we were in her room, and she was sitting at the edge of her bed, hanging her head way over and massaging her scalp to get the blood to go to the ends of her hair shafts. This was to cure her split ends which she, with a shock, had discovered during study hall that day. Well, of course I don't have a date exactly. Not like going to the movies. But he is expecting me. It is a little thrilling to think about what he might be doing, waiting for me. Like is he looking at the clock and wondering, Now what exactly did she look like again?

"I'll call her when I get back," I say. I hope that will be twenty seconds before my father gets home. I hope my whole free time will be taken up with Jimmy. I wonder what his last name is. And middle.

I go into the bathroom, take a look at myself. I might need to get a blunt cut, but of course I can't do that now. I comb my hair, arrange my bangs by ratting them a little. There is a cowlick off to the side of my bangs and arranging them is not always easy. But today I do pretty well. I put on a little pink lipstick. Then I take it off. Then I put it on again. I stand back from the mirror to watch my mouth while I talk. "Hello," I say. "Here's your uniform back." Yes. The lipstick is good. "Sure," I tell the mirror. "I can stay."

He is out gassing up a car when I get there. I raise my hand, wave.

"Hi!" he says. "How are you? Warmer?" At first I don't know what he means but then I remember that of course that is how we met, I was near frozen to death.

"Yes, I'm fine now." I hold the uniform out. "I brought it back."

"Great. Thanks."

He takes the nozzle out of the gas tank, starts cleaning the windshield. Well, I don't know what I'm supposed to do. I thought this would all work out naturally. But now I only feel stupid, like a person shoved out onto the bare stage before the show begins. Naked.

"Want to put it in the office for me?"

Now I feel better. I have a thing to do. I'll wait in there.

Just as I get inside, another car pulls up. I look at the clock. If this were one of those old-time plays, I'd say the fates were conspiring against us. I watch Jimmy finish cleaning the windshield. It's a red Cadillac he's working on, and a fat man wearing a hat is sitting behind the wheel and watching him. One thing about people who own fancy cars is they are sort of crazy when it comes to them. They are so particular, like the car is the only one in the world, when if you go down to the lot, you will see six or seven more lined up. I wish it would have been a little, dirty car with a relaxed person inside, so Jimmy could finish faster. Although now I do have some time to get ready.

I take off my coat, sit in his chair, slant my legs to the side. This is how you're supposed to do it, but it's hard to stay that way. Once when I was doing it, my leg started shaking so I had to quick improvise to the crossed-leg position even though that is how prostitutes sit.

I get up to lean against the wall, my hands clasped in front of me. Then I move my hands behind me, lean against them. That's better. It looks more natural. Plus older. My skirt is hanging perfectly over my nylons. There is nothing spilled on my sweater. I take out one hand from behind my back, use it to find the clasp on my pearl solitaire necklace, make sure it's at the very back of my neck. It's a cultured pearl, real. If you rub it on your teeth you can feel the sand from where it used to live.

I hear the sound of the outside bell, look out the window. Another car has pulled into the station! I feel so mad at the driver. It is a woman, staring at herself in the rearview mirror like she has forgotten that what she should be doing is watching to make sure she's ready to pull right up when the person ahead of her is done.

I get out of my pose, go over to look at what's in the candy machine. I like everything there except the peanut-butter crackers.

I pick the order of what I would eat. First place goes to Nestlé's Crunch. Last place to Tootsie Roll.

So there is a hot-beverage machine in here and a candy machine. If there were a sudden blizzard, you would be fine. Really, you could live here, just hang up some curtains and there you are. There is a bathroom and a telephone. He has a hot plate in the back, I saw it when I changed, with some cans of soup by it. Bean and Bacon, which is my favorite also. You could use a mattress on the floor at night.

I look outside again. Jimmy is turned away from me, leaning over an engine. Say you pointed to anything there and said, "What's that?" I'm sure he would know. Even if it were something under something else. There are more or less ten years between us. That is nothing, if you really think about it. After I finished high school, nobody would say a word. And it would be a neat thing, like when he was forty-three, I would be thirty-three. "How old are you?" Twenty-seven. "And your husband?" Thirty-seven. Easy.

The pay phone rings, which makes me jump. I lean out the door. "Jimmy? The phone is ringing!" I could be calling him in to our apartment.

"Could you answer it, please?"

"Me?" I point to myself like a dope, wreck the whole thing.

"Just say 'Mobil Oil' and ask them to hold on."

I pick up the receiver. "Mobil Oil," I say. "May I help you?" I am so nervous for many reasons.

"... Hello?" a woman's voice says.

"Mobil Oil," I say, louder. "Can I help you?"

"Is *Jimmy* there?" she says. I hear a kid yelling in the background. I believe he is saying "Mine" but it is hard to tell since the sound is so long and drawn out. It sounds like someone falling from a cliff.

"Just a minute, please." I'm not sure what to do with the phone. There is no hall table to lay it on. I let it down gradually, leave it hanging there, and go to the door again. "Hey, Jimmy!" I have to yell, but I do it in as dainty a way as I can. "It's for you."

"All right. Tell them just a minute."

Well, it is the team of us.

"I did."

"Okay. Be right there."

I hear noise coming from the phone and I go to stand closer so I can hear. Some entertainment has suddenly arrived.

"What did I tell you?" I hear the woman yelling. "Huh? What did I *tell* you?" There is a silence and then the kid starts bawling loud. She either hit him or took something away from him. "Damn it!" she says. Her voice is like a rope unraveling.

I move away from the phone. Something has just occurred to me that hits like a sock to the stomach. She could be his wife. There could be pans on their stove, her making his dinner.

They could have their wedding album out on the coffee table and look at it often and fondly.

He is coming in now, smiling at me so friendly, and there is no wedding ring on his left hand. And in that moment I decide, I don't care if he is married. I'm staying. It is every woman for herself.

I am sitting in my room thinking I have never seen anyone change so fast as Diane has. She is the kind of person who always looked so done and you never saw her doing it. She had things on her dresser: emery boards, bobby pins, Aqua-Net, makeup, perfume, scarves and barrettes to wear in her hair; but you never saw her using anything and she always looked so good. But now! When I first saw her, I didn't know where to look. In the bad way. Her nails were almost all broken off, and she had not cut them all short, which you are supposed to do if two or more get broken. She had one ring finger long, and on the other hand the thumb; all the rest were broken off short. Her hair was tied back in a low ponytail, not shiny. No makeup except the black rings of eyeliner. I tried to look like I didn't notice anything, but she knew. It was a hurt in her face, saying, "Yes, I know." She had gained some weight, too. I wouldn't say you could call her fat, but she was not the same in that department either. It was not pregnant weight, which according to what I learned you would not see yet anyway; what Diane told me last time we spoke is she is three months. At three months the morning sickness should be thinking about leaving. But if not, eat soda crackers before you even get up to pee.

Dickie looked absolutely the same. Same clothes, same hairdo, same slow grin. I can't say that my father was polite to him, but he didn't kick him out, which is how he used to treat him. There is a bedroom made up for them in the living room out of the sofa. They are out now, buying the groceries we need, for tomorrow. The frank truth is I need some time to get used to how Diane looks, which is why I decided not to go along. My father took them in his car, Dickie is plenty tired of driving. His truck is parked out front. It is the same, too.

I come out into the kitchen, find Ginger hanging up her apron. She is ready to go home for the long weekend. "I wish you could eat Thanksgiving dinner here," I say.

"Do you?" This makes her happy. It's a good thing to let people know how much you like them. It's strange but true that people usually forget to do that, but then when you see how the littlest compliment can make a person sit up lively you say to yourself, oh yeah.

I sit at the kitchen table. "What will you be doing tomorrow?"

"Oh," she turns around, wipes the sink out with a sponge even though it is already clean. "I'll be making dinner. Wayne will be coming with his family. His parents and his two sisters." She is tired already, just talking about it. Behind the veil of her niceness, you can see the other feelings.

"Well, we'll save leftovers here for you."

"Thanks. On Monday, we'll have turkey

sandwiches when you come home from school, how's that?"

Now I am a little nervous. Dickie eats a lot. The turkey might be plumb gone by Monday. I really meant just that we'd be thinking of her. "Well," I say. "Or pie, something like that."

"Right." She looks at her watch. It's a cheap silver one, gaps in the links. I wish I could buy her a new one. I know for Christmas I'm getting her a book. A hardback. "I have to go, Katie. Please tell Diane and Dickie that I enjoyed meeting them."

"I will."

"And tell your father... Well, just Happy Thanksgiving, I guess." She looks at me a little too long and I see that she is thinking about him in the romantic way. Which I guess I had known but hadn't known until now. Facts bump up against me like waves. How she has been fixing herself up more lately. How she leaves at night slowly.

Huh. Him, as a plain man.

Just as Ginger is going out the door, the phone rings. I get an alarmed feeling that it might be Jimmy, although I would also be happy. We had a good time, when I was there. He has a checkers game which we played, I won one, he won one, which of course leaves you with a very satisfied feeling. He said, "Come by again," when I left, which was a relief, since that *was* his wife on the phone. They got married right out of high school, is about all he said. He kind of smiled, saying it. But their son is five years old. So figure it out. That man got trapped like a rat.

"Hello?" I say, and I can actually feel my heart beating in my chest.

"Hi! Where have you been?"

Oh. It's Cynthia.

"I'm sorry," I say. "I forgot to call you back." She phones a few times a day, and if I don't answer or call back right away, why call out the FBI.

"It's okay," she says. And then there is a loud silence. This is one of those friendships where I'll have to do all the talking.

"How's your grandma?" I say.

"She and my mother are going at it right now. Nona got up last night and made three gallons of red sauce."

"What for?"

Cynthia sighs. "Oh, you know, spaghetti, all that stuff. Calzones. Pizza."

"No, I mean, are you having a lot of people over?"

"No. Nobody. Nona just loves to cook. It's her only thing. My god, if *people* are coming over for dinner! Then she makes about two *hundred* gallons. She gets all excited. She rubs her hands together and says, 'Ah, business, she's-a pickin' up!' "

"So what's wrong if she cooks?" I ask.

"She has bad heart problems. Congestive failure. Sometimes she's just not supposed to get up. Her legs are swollen up again like crazy. You should see them. If you poke them with your finger, the mark stays."

This is not something I would buy a ticket for.

"She got up when everyone was sleeping. I don't know, three in the morning or something, that's how she does it. She's really quiet, I have to say that. She lights a candle, cooks by that."

"Really?" Now this is something I would like to see. Cynthia's grandmother, dressed in a robe and slippers, her hair wild and sticking out all over, stirring sauce by the light of a big white candle. Like a good witch. The skins of onions and garlic all over the kitchen counter. She would stir and stir, squint into the pot, sprinkle her spices in. I'll bet she puts wine in, right from the bottle, I saw an Italian grandmother do that once in a movie. The bottle was in its own basket. Nona only uses her own spices, I remember Cynthia telling me that, that she grows spices in the summer. Plus tomatoes, which she cans. These are skills I don't know anything about. I don't think many people know how to can, although seniors in Miss Woods's class do. I never saw basil growing. If Cynthia and I are still friends in the summer, that is one thing I would like to see: Nona's garden, with things you can eat just growing for free. You want something? Just go out in the backyard and pick it. She has lettuce coming up from the dirt, raw peas.

"She's up there *screaming* now," Cynthia says. "At my mother. Can't you hear her?"

I listen carefully. "No."

"I'll hold the phone out," Cynthia says. "Listen."

I listen again. "No," I say. "I can't hear."

Nothing.

"Cynthia?" I say.

Nothing.

Well, look at this. *"Cynthia!"*

"What?" she says. "Did you hear?"

"No." I'm getting tired of this conversation.

"Oh well, you wouldn't understand it anyway, it's all Italian."

"Your mother speaks Italian?"

"Oh yeah. Nona gets her mad enough, she'll spout Italian all day long."

Well. A dent in Mrs. O'Connell.

"Can you come over tomorrow?" Cynthia asks.

"It's Thanksgiving."

"I know. But before dinner."

"I don't think so. My sister's here and everything."

"Really? I didn't know you had a sister. What's she like?"

The door opens, and I hear Diane's voice. Then she is in the kitchen putting grocery bags on the counter. She waves at me but there is nothing in it, no life.

"I'll have to talk to you later," I say.

"Is she right there?" Cynthia asks, like we have secrets together against Diane.

"No. I just have to go."

"But can you come over on Friday?"

"I guess," I say. "All right."

"I'll teach you piano."

A brightening in me. "Okay."

My father comes in the kitchen, his face shut

down. Well, here we are, back to the old days, just like that. I don't know what it is between the two of them. It is like they are allergic to each other.

"Hey," I say.

No one answers.

"Need any help carrying things in?"

"We got it all," Dickie says. He looks like he is ready to blow up with uncomfortableness. I feel sorry for him. I wish I could tell him to go in my room, but that would be taking sides and my father would just get madder. When he is like this, he welcomes more to keep him going.

"I'll just go get the mail," I say.

My father starts putting groceries away. I pity the shelves he will slam the cans down onto.

Diane goes into the living room and sits on the sofa. She is holding one hand with the other, rubbing her knuckles. I keep thinking, inside her is that little baby. Held right in her center. Surrounded by magic liquid. Listening for her body to tell it every single thing to do.

Dickie comes in and sits beside her and it's like he isn't even there.

"Hey, Dickie," I say. "Want to get the mail with me?" It's a country-type mailbox, out at the curb. It has a red flag to put up when you want to tell the mailman to stop and take something. I don't know why we have a country mailbox when this is the suburbs, but who knows why they do what they do here? I could show Dickie how it works.

"No thanks, Katie."

He wants to help Diane, but I can tell him he might as well give up right now.

I go outside and it is such a relief to be out of that house. There is the sky, which has nothing to do with any of this. I'd thought we were going to make pies and it would be a little fun. I'd imagined my father and Dickie wearing aprons too, and it would be cute-funny, like when the men on TV cook and do things all wrong which only makes their wives say, Oh HONEY, and love them more. But no.

Well, there is some mail, but it is all window mail. Bills. But then I see a small envelope, purple. I turn it over, feel so happy at the sight of a letter from Cherylanne. One thing she is still doing in her own way is being there, I have not lost her after all.

I come inside, put the other mail on the kitchen table, go into my room and shut the door quietly. I use my scissors to open the envelope neatly. There are three pages!

Dear Katie,

Well, you have hit the jackpot this time. I cannot believe you have a nineteen-year-old boyfriend, older than mine!! I am not jealous, but I have to say aren't you sort of young for this? And do you know what you are doing?? Don't think I am being like your mother. Sorry. I mean like a parent. But you do have to be careful when they are sooooo much older. I have heard some stories which I will tell you another time. But of course there is also a lot of romance in May-December relationships, which is something I told you about a long time ago. Although then you did not get it.

Todd and I are as in love as we can be. We have not talked once about breaking up or even had one fight. All we do is plan, plan, plan for our next fun event. So everything is fine there. Although I have noticed someone else watching me and it is hard not to get a little interested. But I am not that kind. Eric Uppman is his name. A blond boy, plus center on the basketball team. Which is coming up.

You had a lot of questions!!! I will answer as many as I can. I do know the answer to all of them, but we may need to do the installment plan, because I have a lot of homework, especially stupid history, which who cares about it.

Number one. Soul kissing is just the same as French kissing, except when Negroes do it, it is soul. Soul and French are the same exact thing, which is you use tongues, which I am sure you have heard of. It is not as hard as it sounds, but maybe the first time you do it you might feel like vomiting. Which even I did, if you can imagine, but of course that was long ago. Anyway, first: RELAX!!! Just pretend beautiful Motsart piano music is in your head playing "Alone at Last." And let your hair fall gently along your back because one thing is they like to put their hands in it. (Make sure it is COMBED and CLEAN and of course as always it is a good place to put perfume.) You will feel their tongue come in. Wait, first, make sure your mouth is soft and easy to open up. Do not keep it clamped together like they feel they need a can opener. They hate that and if you do it you can be sure the next day they will be telling their friends you are a prude. (You don't *want to be a prude. Also you don't want to be easy. It takes some work to balance all this!!) But anyway, then you will feel their tongue come in your mouth sort of squirming around like a snake and a little spitty. This is the part where you might feel queasy but do NOT LET ON!! This is so important, Katie, especially with such an older guy. You have to move your tongue, too. Try just figure 8s. That move is a good one which they seem to enjoy.*

Two. Yes, you are right, you must let them stop kissing first. Or it could hurt their male ego. But of course you can breathe!! Otherwise, there would be plenty of dead girls lying around, ha ha! Just through your nose. You can do it easier than you think. I recommend practicing with a pillow.

Katie, I have just looked at my watch and it is too late for me to finish. I will write more later. It is more interesting there now isn't it???? See, I told you. I can't believe he looks like Superman, is that really true or are you maybe exaggerating just a little bit?

Now I must go and I am eager to hear how you do with Jimmy. Of course you are right NOT to tell your father, who would probably blow his brains out.

Love,

Cherylanne

Maybe later Diane will feel better and I will ask her to check all the things that Cherylanne said. One thing about Diane is that when she's in the mood to talk, she always tells me the truth. Unlike me, who has now begun to lie like crazy. I don't know when it started, but it's beginning to get out of control. Like those cans you buy in the joke shop and you open the lid and *wham*.

I hear a knock on the door, look around for a place to hide the letter. That's all I need is for him to see it. I slide it into my pillowcase, say, "Come in."

It's Diane, her face an apology.

"Hi," I say.

"Come on, let's walk the dog. Then we'll come back and make some pies."

Well, she has rallied, as they say. Maybe she is already starting to be a mother because she can't help herself, her body is taking over, and so she is thinking about someone else's feelings. That's what mothers do, is always get in back of the line. "No," they say, holding up their hand, "I'm fine."

We go outside and I am hooking up Bridgette to her leash when I see another note in the bushes. I'm not sure whether I should tell Diane. But she sees it herself, and she walks over to it, pulls it out, shows me. "Well, what's *this?*" she says, smiling. "Have you been getting love notes?"

I shake my head, glance quickly across the street.

"What's wrong?" She looks at the note again, then back at me. The fun has all evaporated. "Can I read it?"

I come up to her, say quietly, "It's not a love note."

"Yeah, all right. Can I read it?"

I shrug. I've wanted to tell her, but now I'm not so sure. For one thing, Diane is not quite Diane.

She reads the note, hands it to me. In the usual print is this: WE KNOW WHERE YOU'VE BEEN AND WHAT YOU'VE BEEN DOING.

"What the hell is this?" Diane asks. "What are they talking about?"

"I don't know," I say. "The kids across the street put notes there. I don't know what it means." Jimmy, I'm thinking. They saw me with him. They know just how I feel about him. I feel like my privacy is a white place where they've wiped their dirty hands.

Diane reads the note again, then crumples it and puts it in her pocket. We start walking, and she says, "What did the other notes say?"

"They're all different. Just... stuff."

"I wonder why they're doing that."

"I don't know. I didn't do anything."

Diane looks back down the street. "Is that the house? The white one right across from ours?"

"Yeah."

"Want to pay them a little visit?"

"No." I say this too fast. She doesn't like what a coward I am. She got the adventure genes in the family.

"Well, I think we should. Maybe a little later. Maybe around three A.M."

"I just ignore them." Not true. I always feel really bad.

Diane takes Bridgette's leash from my hand, reins her in closer. "Sometimes, Katie, you need to take a little control of your own life. When it's time to say *stop*, you need to say *stop*. It can happen when you first move somewhere that people like to give you a little test."

"Right."

"So you need to let them know who you are, that you'll stand up for yourself."

"Okay."

We are walking exactly together. I feel better just because now she knows about the notes too. It's really all I needed.

"Diane?"

"Yeah."

"Did you know your baby can hear you?"

She looks over at me, and I see a glimmer of her old beauty in the line of her cheekbone, the blackness of her hair. "Is that right?"

"Yes."

She looks away. "Well, I hope he doesn't hear too well. There sure hasn't been anything good for him to hear."

I consider whether or not to tell her about the notebook of things about babies. I have given it a title: *Facts About the Team of You and Your Baby*. Probably there will be a better time later.

Still, "Your baby doesn't care what you say," I tell her. "Anything is fine. He just loves you already. Your voice. Even your body sounds. Like your heart. That *lub, dub,* sound. It sounds like that, *lub, dub*. He loves that."

She sighs. "Oh, Katie."

"What?" Her look is like she has said turn the light on and I have started lifting up rugs to find the switch. Like I don't get anything.

"Forget it," she says. "Nothing."

We stop talking. It looks like this walk will cheer up only one of us: Bridgette is happy as could be. Stones are a whole show to her. She sniffs each one like it's breaking her heart to leave it; like later, when no one is interfering, she'll come back and visit it the right way.

Before I go to sleep, I think about making the pies and how it would have been different if my mother were here. Well, for one thing they would have turned out. And sometimes someone would have smiled. She would have had some music on, probably her Perry Como album. I like him, too. He seems like such a nice man and I understand he used to only be a barber.

I close my eyes and think of my mother in an outfit where I get to touch everything. I like to do this. I make up outfits of my choice. Last time it was a dance dress I made up, a filmy white thing with rhinestones on the bodice, and thin, thin straps that are called spaghetti. Tonight I make her wearing a blue fancy suit. A square, button jacket and a straight skirt. It's a mohair suit. There is a scarf with it, tucked in rich at the neck. And a pin on her shoulder, a peacock pin with many jewels in the tail. "That's a diamond," she says, when I touch it. "That's a ruby. That's a sapphire." When I ask are they real, she laughs and says yes of course, and that she is saving that pin for me when we meet up again. She is wearing a little round hat. Nylons and blue matching high heels. She is happy.

So tomorrow is Thanksgiving. In everyone's oven will be one dead turkey. I used to like taking walks on Thanksgiving afternoon, thinking you could walk up any sidewalk to any door and knock on it and when it opened, turkey smell. Even if the people don't speak English. But now I have to say I am not much looking forward to Thanksgiving. Our table will be small and quiet. I don't think a single person but me will want the wishbone.

Friday afternoon, I am sitting in Father Compton's church when I hear him coming up behind me. I can tell it's him from the wheeze in his nose. I turn around and smile. I would like to have a word with him.

He is a good kind of priest because he sees that, without my saying anything. He sits in the pew opposite me, nods. "How are you, Katie?" I've got all the time in the world, he is saying.

"Okay." Good, because I need to talk to you, I am saying.

"Paying us a visit today?"

"Yes, sir."

He sits still, waits.

I clear my throat, smile again. "Could I ask you something?"

He nods, serious.

"Okay. So... okay, I'll just say it. Did you ever have a time in your life when you lied a lot?" Well, now there is a jump of fear in me because what if I am wrong about his character?

But he just thinks for awhile, staring off over my shoulder. Then, looking back at me, "Yes."

I wait.

He raises an eyebrow.

I clench one fist, keep my mouth shut.

"But you're not here to talk about me, are you?" he finally says.

"No, sir."

"Well, then." He looks at his watch. "Would you like to come into my office and talk there for a little bit? It's more private. And I have a box of chocolate-covered cherries someone gave me that I'll never finish by myself."

I shiver a little like a breeze has gone down my neck. It's from the pure relief of him. I say yes, I would like to go to his office. While I'm following him there, it comes to me that nobody gave him those chocolates. He bought them for himself, but he's going to share with me. What they ought to do is make him pope. I sigh loudly, happy. He turns toward me, checks my face, then turns away again, continues his slow, bent-over walk toward his office. Yes, his back is saying. Right this way. The language of the body can be such a gentle thing.

Riding my bike to Cynthia's house, I think about what I told Father Compton. I don't know if it was such a good idea. Although he was very nice all the way till the end, I wonder if after I left he didn't close his door and lean against it, saying, "Boy!" Or maybe "Mother of God!" What he mostly said is that lying hurt people. Maybe not at first, but eventually it hurt people, especially the one telling the lie. He talked about a surface being eroded and how that changes the character of a thing and I looked into his eyes like I was listening really hard to all he was saying, and I was listening, but I also was thinking about how amazingly old he is and didn't priests have a retirement rule? He said it really was true about oh what tangled webs we weave, that when you start lying, it just gets more and more complicated. I didn't tell him exactly what I was lying about. I said I had exaggerated some things about a person I cared for. And that I had lied about my age. He said there was also a way of lying by *not* saying things, sins of omission. That was scary. I just nodded, didn't say anything. I was thinking, what if he's a mind reader. What if he knows *everything,* like when I imagined Frenching with Jimmy and how our looks at each other would be so soft when we were done kissing. One thing I need to find out is what do you do after the kiss, like does the girl put her head on his shoulder or what? And can you swallow?

I never did get to ask Diane anything. I didn't show her Cherylanne's letter and I didn't tell her about Jimmy. She seemed so taken up the whole time, so complicated about herself there was not really any room in her for anyone else. I don't think things are going so good with her and Dickie. He is like a puppy and she is like the one saying, "I *told* you no *an*imals!" She said she would write more often and I said I would too. Maybe on paper we can say some things. My father sort of hugged her when she left, but it was too late, it was like they were only hurting each other, touching. During Thanksgiving dinner, she told him about the baby and the words were like a package laid on the table that no one was about to open. My father looked at Dickie, then at Diane; he asked when it would be born and that was that. She and Dickie left this morning earlier than they said they would and I'll bet the inside of that truck is solid quiet.

When I left Father Compton's office I said thank you and he asked did I feel better? I said yes. He said something they have in the Catholic religion is confession, where people can say all that they did in detail, and it is all forgiven. Cherylanne once warned me about this. She said Catholics try to capture you. I told Father Compton I knew about confession but that I didn't exactly believe a man could forgive a person for all they did wrong, especially if it was not done to them. He said no, it was God doing the forgiving. I said Oh, but what I was thinking was well then why not take the direct route? I wish God were realer and would come to town once in awhile. I wish I could see His face, which I understand shines so hard you can't look at it, but I wish I could look at it and say, Well, not to be rude, but could you just tell me exactly why some things happen? I could have just a short list of questions. And probably He could give me a heavenly explanation that I would say OH! to, and then feel so much better for the rest of my life. It would be no sweat for Him and it would mean so much to me. He is stingy, when you think about it.

I hit a bump suddenly and my bottom bangs hard against the bicycle seat. I need to pay attention or I'll end up falling, which would be pretty embarrassing. Of course it is pretty embarrassing anyway, being my age and riding a bike. To say nothing of freezing cold. If Jimmy wasn't too busy, I'll bet he would have given me a ride. I'm going to visit him again tomorrow. I'm using my new brush rollers tonight and I'm going to leave them in until morning even if they kill my head.

Nona is in bed with a tattered cookbook. When Cynthia and I go in to say hello, she smiles at me and puts the book face down on her lap so she doesn't lose her place. "Hey, it's-a my girlfriend!" she says. "You are my girlfriend, right?"

I shrug. "Okay."

"Come here!"

I come closer, stand beside her.

"Sit!" she says, patting the bed with her bent-up fingers.

I sit down beside her. I smell Vicks VapoRub.

She pulls the covers off her legs, scowls furiously at them. Her ankles are swollen, about twice the size they should be, and the swelling extends partway up her leg. "You see?" she says.

I nod. It's creepy, looking at her legs. It makes my fingers feel weak.

"That's-a the problem. Right there."

"Sorry," I say.

She crooks her finger at me, and I lean in

closer. "You know what's-a whiskey?" she asks quietly.

"Yes." Nona has a little mustache. I never noticed before. It's just a little at the corners, like bullfighter guys have sometimes.

"You bring me some whiskey, I'm-a gonna pay you. Fifty dollar!"

I smile.

"Ha! That's a lot, no?"

"Yes, ma'am."

"You bring me some whiskey in a jar like-a perfume. I'm-a pay you."

I smile again, say nothing, look over at Cynthia, who is standing across the room, scratching her elbow and watching Nona's television. I don't think she can hear what's going on.

"I can't get whiskey," I tell Nona.

She sits back, sighs.

"I'm too young," I say.

She leans forward again. "No, no, no. Stupido, huh? You steal from-a you house. You got-a whiskey in you house!"

"No, ma'am."

She stares at me. Blinks. "You gotta no whiskey?"

"I don't think so."

"Whatta you got?"

"You mean liquor?"

She nods. "Yeah, yeah, that's-a right, liquor." She sounds a little like a lady gangster.

"I don't think we have anything." I really can't remember ever seeing liquor in our house.

"You look," she says. "And if-a you find him... " She raises her eyebrows up and down. They are mostly white, but there are a few stray dark hairs from how she used to be.

"Okay, I'll look."

She squeezes her eyes shut, happy, pats my arm harder than you would think she could. "I like-a you friend!" she shouts at Cynthia. She is smiling so hard you can see where her teeth end. I have no idea why Nona likes me so much. But I believe her. And I like that she likes me. It makes you feel good when somebody who's so mean to other people favors you.

Cynthia smiles too, and in the curves of her cheeks I see the resemblance. It's like a photo of the two of them, one over the other, and all of a sudden I have an idea of what Nona looked like as a girl. These yanks into someone's personal past, that's the kind of history I like. Not wars, but who was your grandmother and what did she dream of? Did she walk up stairs to where she lived and what did it smell like and what was she wearing and who were her neighbors?

On the way to Cynthia's bedroom, I tell her I need to pee. She shows me to a small bathroom that is, of all things, inside her mother's bedroom! This is the most deluxe thing I have ever seen. If you want to go in the middle of the night, three steps from the bed and bingo, you are there. There is a lot of powder blue and lace in the bathroom, the faint smell of a good perfume in the air. The wallpaper is tiny blue flowers against a cream-colored background. It's very nice. It makes me want to read in there. I might have a bathroom just like this someday. I appreciate Cynthia bringing me here. I guess she likes it, too, and she is wanting to say, "Here, look at this," without really saying it.

When I am finished and I reach for the toilet paper, I see that the roll is empty. "Cynthia?" I call softly.

Nothing.

"Cynthia?"

"Yeah?" I hear, and it is about the most welcome sound I have ever heard.

"I need some toilet paper," I say. "There's none in here."

"Okay," she says, and then, "Mooommmm!"

Well now, there. There is the most *un*welcome sound. I feel my face getting warm, like a fever. I put my knees together, fold my hands in my naked lap.

After awhile, I hear Cynthia's mother outside the bathroom door. "Katie?" Her voice is kind of like a birdcall. *Ta-wit! Ta-wit!* This is my own joke, which I have just made up on the spot. I smile to myself, answer, "Yes, ma'am?"

"Are you in there?"

I roll my eyes so hard I'm scared she might hear it. This woman should be a display at a museum. Press this button to see something unbelievable.

"Yes, ma'am."

"And you need some tissue, is that it?"

"Uh-huh."

"Well, all right. What I'm going to do is just throw some in, all right? And then you just reach out and grab it, how's that?"

I wait to see if she is going to tell me what to do after I get the tissue. But no, she must think that part I'll be able to figure out all by myself.

"Okay," I call out. I think, I'm never coming here again, unless she's gone. Want to come over? Cynthia will say and I'll say sure, as long as your mother is in Timbuktu.

The door opens a crack and I hear Cynthia's mother say, "Now I'm *not* looking, okay?" And she throws in a roll of blue toilet tissue.

"Got it?"

The bathroom is small. Where does she think it might have gone?

"Yes, I do. Thank you," I listen to see if I can hear her walk away. I would like to finish up in peace. But I don't hear anything. That's the thing with wall-to-wall. Maybe I will not have that.

When I come out of the bathroom I see Cynthia's mother standing at her dresser, arms crossed. "Everything okay?"

"Yes, ma'am."

We pass each other and I am almost to Cynthia's room when I hear her call me. I go back to the bathroom and she is standing beside the toilet-paper dispenser. "Oh, there you are," she says, smiling like we are best friends. "I just wanted to tell you—I don't know how you do it in your house, dear—but here, we put the tissue on so that it comes off the *top* of the roll. That way, you see, it's easier to get to. And you can make a pretty little point out of the first sheet here." She has actually folded the first square of tissue so it makes a *V*. "In your nicer hotels, you'll see that," she says. "That's how you know."

She is such a pretty woman. And so even though I know she is wrong I look at her face and some part of me thinks she must be right. And that part of me feels ashamed.

"Okay," I tell her, and I go into Cynthia's room. "Your mother is really crazy," I tell her.

"Why?"

I think about trying to answer, but then say, "Never mind." Maybe Cynthia just needs to spend more time with normal people. I will give her time, and soon she will be asking me, "What can I *do* about her?" We will try to come up with things, and that will make our friendship stronger. "A friend in trouble, and the friendship's double," Cherylanne used to say. She made it up herself. Which she also used to tell me every time she said it.

I sit in Cynthia's flowered chair, hold her pillows against my stomach tight. "Guess what?" I say.

"What?"

"I have a boyfriend." The words are so delicious, like floating donuts.

"You do? Who?"

"Well," I say. "He's a little bit older, but we think it can work." At the same time I say this,

I have a vision of Father Compton smacking his forehead. I feel a little badly, but I have let this slip out and it's too late to stop now.

"What's he look like?" Cynthia asks.

Well. We'd better check the time. It could take hours just to do his blue, blue eyes.

Taylor Sinn is in my gym class, too, and we have been made partners for counting each other's sit-ups. We are doing those tests for the president to see if we are all too out of shape or what. I guess he is worried about us American youths and he thinks the Russian kids are all ready for the Olympics, just walking around restless in their streets, their fists hitting their palms, saying, "Lemme at 'em." Miss Sweet is delirious with joy because she gets to carry her clipboard from kid to kid, writing her brains out.

I am holding Taylor's ankles and she is doing sit-ups like it is no big deal and she could do them all day long. I am done with mine. I did sixteen, and cheated on half of them because I bent my knees, plus I did not exactly touch my elbows to them except when Miss Sweet walked over and stood by me. All I could see were her knees, which look athletic and which I truly hate. I would like to draw faces on them, two frowns. Taylor said she'd tell Miss Sweet I did fifty sit-ups if I wanted, who cared? I could get away with it, too, because it's the honor system, the partner tells what the other girl did. But I said no, because really even to say sixteen was cheating and why push it? So Taylor is up to sixty and I am frankly getting bored counting. Her shirt is tucked into her gym shorts which is something you don't see too often. On her first day she wore a belt, too, which Miss Sweet of course had a heart attack about and made her take it off IMMEDIATELY. It actually looked really good. If I did that there would be a dent with my belly hanging out above and below. I suppose I am what you would call a little chubby. Taylor's stomach is flat, flat, flat. I don't know how she does it. Although looking at her do all these sit-ups, maybe that's how.

"Do you do these at home?" I ask, at eighty-one.

"Yeah." Her gorgeous hair is tied back in a low ponytail today, a wide black ribbon on it. Also her outfit that she wore today is black, I saw it in English. She looked like she should be the teacher. No. She looked like she should be the rich mother, wearing gold hoop earrings, come to talk to the teacher about her child, who is a budding genius.

"I'm going to stop at a hundred," Taylor says. "This is boring as shit."

"Oh," I say. Imagine having a choice about when to stop.

"You look like a model," I tell her.

"I am."

"You are?"

"Yeah."

She is not even out of breath.

"Like they take pictures of you?"

"Yeah, I do that. And I do live modeling. For Steinbeck's."

I know what she means. There is a wall in that fancy department store where they have all their models' pictures hanging. All those girls look as if they can't be real. But of course they are, and here is one of them and I am holding down her ankles.

"I guess you have to look old to be a model," I say.

"You have to look like a model to be a model."

"Yeah. That's what I mean."

"One hundred," she says, leaning back on her elbows. "Right?"

I don't know. I quit counting. "Right," I say.

I go over to tell Miss Sweet the number, and she says, "*Who* did that?"

"Taylor Sinn."

"Oh," she says, looking over at her. "Okay." She can tell by Taylor's body that it is true. I can see right now that Miss Sweet would like Taylor to be her pet but I've got news for her. Taylor thinks the same thing about every teacher, no matter who they are. And it is not that she wishes she could be their pet.

When I am dressed, Taylor comes to sit beside me on the locker-room bench. "What's your name again?"

"Katie."

"You ever go by Katherine?"

I shake my head.

"You should. It's more you."

"Oh." This feels like a compliment, but I'm not sure, it could be a joke. I smile like I get it either way.

"You want to go to Woolworth's after school?"

"I have to ride the bus."

"I could give you a ride home. My sister drives. She comes to get me every day."

"You have a sister?"

"Yeah. She's a junior. She's at my old school. She models, too. You've probably seen her in the newspaper, maybe catalogs."

Well, two in one family. That is so amazing. I bet they have makeup like crazy. I bet they have a big drawer, just stuffed with every single thing. When they sit at the dinner table together, what can that be like? The two of them so beautiful, just sitting side by side and cutting their meat, their hair hanging down their backs.

"I have to go somewhere today," I say. "But I could go with you tomorrow."

"All right," she says. And then, "I liked your paper that Mrs. Brady read to us in English. About 'Birches.' That was really good."

I smile, feel a bubble of happiness rising up in me that makes my mouth tight. I could be on the verge of having two friends, just like that. Plus Jimmy. This is the way things work sometimes, that good things get ideas from each other, say, Well now let's go ahead and let her have it all.

Jimmy is reading the newspaper at his desk and he takes a moment to look up when I come in. Then, "Hey!" he says. "Katie!" He leans back in his chair and smiles and I can see I was dead right about everything. Sometimes your brain will liven things up for you, make things a little exaggerated to keep up your interest in life, but not this time. He is just like I remembered and more.

I am so glad he seems happy to see me. I never said I was coming. This was a surprise visit. I thought he might be glad to see me, but then the last little way before I got here I had to all of a sudden consider the alternative. And I had planned that if he looked annoyed I would say I'd been sent to buy something. Valvoline.

"You're not planning to skate today, are you? I think it's way too warm."

"No. I just had some time and I was going this way. I thought I'd come and visit."

"Good."

And now, *blam,* I cannot think of one thing to say. I have thought so much about all the things I want to tell him, but that was when I was imagining us in the middle of our relationship, when we are used to kissing. I can't even look at his mouth now, which is how far we are from the real thing.

"How was school?" he asks.

Well, there. A subject. I start to tell him and before I get the first sentence out, he pulls up a chair for me. I am welcome here. I sit down like a lady, watch his face while I talk. He really listens, and he laughs out loud a lot, especially when I tell him about home ec. Today Miss Woods slipped on vegetable oil. "Imagine if I were a guest in your home!" she yelled at the girl who had spilled it.

"And how was your day?" I ask.

His face changes. "Not much to it, I'm afraid."

I wait.

He looks at me, widens his eyes, smiles. His hands are in his pockets, fists balled up. I think he is a little embarrassed and this hurts my feelings on his behalf.

"Well," I say. "What did you have for breakfast?"

He laughs. "Coffee."

"That's all?"

"Yeah, that's all." He looks out the window. "If I want breakfast, I get it out."

"But you're married." Oh, if it were me. Golden pancakes stacked up high, butter melting into the real maple syrup. A blue-and-white-checked napkin tucked into his ironed shirt. A little flower in a little vase. The newspaper folded by his fork, but he wouldn't read it because we would be in love and talking to beat the band.

"Hey," he says, suddenly. "You want to see something?"

I nod.

A car pulls in and Jimmy gets up to go outside. "Wait here," he says. And I think, Oh don't worry. I'll wait. For about forever.

What he shows me is a car under a sheet that is in one of the bays of the garage. He pulls off the cover and there it is, a little white sports car. A convertible. There is a little cage over the headlights and the grill looks like shark teeth.

"What is it?"

"A fifty-four," he says, speaking like we are in a giant cathedral.

"That's the kind of car?"

He looks at me. "It's a 'Vette!"

I stare at him.

"A Corvette! A Blue Flame Six!"

"Oh. Right."

"You've never seen a Corvette?"

"I don't know."

"Well, you probably haven't seen one of these." He walks around the car, opens the passenger door. "Want to sit in it?"

"All right." I get in, and he closes the door behind me. It's so low and round in here. It was probably a good deal, it only has plastic for windows on the side.

He gets in, puts his hands on the steering wheel. He has a smile I'll bet he's not aware of. We are in the French countryside, on our way to a picnic with wine and cheese and *du chocolat.*

"Should we go for a ride?" I ask.

He looks at me like I have said, “Can I kill you?”

“Not in the *win*ter!”

“Oh.”

“Katie, this car... You want to treat something like this with the utmost respect.”

“Uh-huh.”

“It’s... Well, it’s one of the first ones, for one thing. They only made three hundred in 1953. Made a little over 3,500 of these.”

“Right.”

One thing I admire is a man who has a handle on the facts. Tomorrow I will get a book out of the library so I can say my own things about cars back to him. And I’ll write down what he said about this one. *’Vette,* I think to myself. It sounds nice, kind of exciting, too. “Does your wife like to ride in here?” I ask.

There, a curtain again over his eyes. “She doesn’t know I have it. She doesn’t like cars. She’d kill me if she knew about this one.”

“Well,” I say. “I love it.” And starting right now, I really do. “Does the radio work?” I say. Later, I will say, “Can I see the engine?” and that will give me about two thousand points, I know it.

I am sitting in my room doing homework when I hear a rustle outside. I go to the window and see Greg out in the dark, his arm stuck in the bushes. I am so tired of this. Why isn't he? I open the window and he jumps back, looks up at me. His eyes are like a rabbit's in the headlights. "Why don't you just hand it to me?" I say. "It'll save us both some work."

He is so embarrassed, I swear I can feel the heat of his face from here.

"What?" he says. "I don't have anything."

"It's the note I'm talking about. You know, the one in your hand? With all the misspellings?"

He starts to leave, and I say, "I think that's enough now. If you do this again, I'll need to do something about it. And believe me, I am a creative person." My inside parts are looking at each other like, *What????* They are flat amazed that I am saying these things. I feel split in two, with the new self saying, Step back, Jack; and the old self saying, Yikes. But the main feeling is just plain good. I am changing for the better right on the spot, right in front of myself, like the chrysalis who had no idea, who was resigned to the cocoon until he got the wings.

"Go to hell," Greg says, stomping off, but the air has left that boy's balloon. He won't do this anymore, that's all his "go to hell" means. He will go home now and wonder what to do with the note and feel like a jerk. He will shrug around inside himself and finally watch TV or something, but it will keep nudging him, this little defeat; and I'm glad.

I close the window, sit down on my bed. I can't believe what I just found in me. But I think I know who put it there. When you have a big love, it's like a powerful blanket, laid down on your land, warming you and protecting you. Something like that. I get out my poetry notebook. History can wait. Today two kids fell asleep in Mr. Spurlock's class and he didn't even notice until one started snoring.

I am dreaming that I am late for class. The bell is ringing and ringing and I am standing still in the hall like I am paralyzed. Then it comes to me that it's the phone I'm hearing. I start to get out of bed, but then hear my father answering it. There is a long pause. I open my door, see his back. He is wearing underwear and a T-shirt; he didn't take the time to put a robe on. His arms are crossed; he is using his head to hold the phone. I guess he's cold. I think about getting his robe for him, but he might get embarrassed. I'll just wait. I look at my clock: 1:30. Who would be calling now? Whoever it is, they don't know my father. Or maybe this is an emergency. It's funny, the first thing I think is, Oh, that would be interesting, an emergency, I wonder what it is.

And then I get ashamed of myself. And then I think, Diane.

I come out into the hall. "Dad?"

He doesn't move.

"Dad?"

He turns around, holds up a finger. "Get me my robe," he says quietly, still listening.

I get his robe off the end of his bed, bring it to him. After he puts it on, I go to sit on the floor in front of him to see if I can tell what's going on. "Are you talking to Diane?" I say.

He puts his hand over the mouthpiece. "Katie, just wait. No. It's Dickie." Then, into the phone, "Well, I'll be there. I'll leave in just a little while."

Some quiet, his face working on something.

"No, I think I should. I'll be there as soon as I can. I'll call you from the road for directions when I get closer."

He hangs up, sighs, looks at me. "She lost the baby."

Oh, this soft punch, right to the center. I miss that baby I never met, and I feel so sorry for Diane. She must be lying pale on the pillow, empty and still.

"Is she okay?"

"Well, she's in some goddamn Mexican hospital."

I think of a Mexican nurse, straightening with the insult. He doesn't know about Mexican hospitals. "Are they bad?"

"They're not here," he scoffs.

"But are they bad?"

"Katie, listen to me now. I'm going to get her, and bring her home. And I'm going to call Ginger right now to come and stay with you. All right?"

I nod. It's too late. Ginger's asleep. The buses don't run now. But he is on the phone, dialing her number.

"Go to your room," he says.

Now, why?

But I go.

I get under my covers, think, how did that baby look? Why did it leave? I wonder if Diane's stomach hurts, if she is crying. I would guess not. I would guess she is staring straight ahead. Dickie will come in and say, "Your father's coming to take you home." She will say, "The hell he is." I could save my father a trip. I know she will never come back with him. Whatever pain she has about this baby she will just add to my father's pile. It's how the two of them are together, and I for one have given up hoping it will ever change.

My door opens, and my father says, "I've got to go pick Ginger up. I'll be back."

"Can I come?"

"No. Go to sleep."

"I can't sleep now!"

He stands there for a moment, the light from the hall outlining him like he is an alien. Then, "Fine," he says. "Put on your coat. I want to get moving."

Well, so do I. That's why I asked to come.

Ginger lives in a little house on a narrow

street. It's a white house with window boxes, empty now, but waiting. There is a small porch in front with a wicker rocker on it, a mailbox hanging a little crooked at the side of her door. A deep yellow light is on to say welcome.

We pull up to the curb, and a dog starts barking. I didn't know Ginger had a dog. He's a big one, too; I see his head at the window.

We get out of the car and ring the doorbell and now the dog really goes berserk, barking hoarsely and hurling himself at the door like he thinks he's the star of a cop show.

"Bones!" Ginger yells. "Stop that!"

Bones! Well, now that is one dog's name I have never heard before.

She opens the door, yanks at Bones's collar. "Come on in," she says. "I'll be ready in a minute. Don't worry about him—he's all talk."

The dog is a skinny one, who looks like he has a lot of Great Dane in him. I see where he got his name. His ribs look like he is wearing them as a vest.

"I just got him a couple of weeks ago," Ginger says. "Poor thing, you should have seen him."

I don't want to hurt her feelings, but he is nothing to write home about now.

"I'll get his leash," she says, "and then we can go."

Oh, of course. She has to bring the dog, she won't be back for a few days. Well, I'm going to be sitting in the front seat on the way home, that's for sure. Bones does not seem exactly pleased to make my acquaintance. He is sniffing me, but he has planted himself far enough away that he has to stretch out his neck to do so. This is a dog's way of saying, "Don't get any ideas."

"Hey," I say to him, friendly. "*I* got a dog."

He is sniffing one place in particular on my hand. Probably it's Bridgette he smells, and probably he's saying to me, "No kidding."

I take a look at Ginger's living room, off to the side of the hall. She is not a wealthy woman, I can tell. But she has fixed up what she has so comfortably it makes you want to stay there awhile. There is a jewel-colored afghan draped over the back of an old sofa, books neatly lined up in the cases along the walls, plants along the top shelf. She has a lot of books. I can see from here that they're nearly all paperbacks so they don't look quite as pretty as what you see in magazine pictures, but they do their job just fine, which is to make you feel satisfied. It's a cozy thing to know you have so many books, that you can at any moment walk over and browse in your own house.

There are some pictures on the wall, mostly flowers, it looks like, and the white curtains at the window are clean and ruffled. She has a rug with giant roses on it, a rocking chair with yellow corduroy cushions. There is another chair completely covered by a spread, so I guess its show-off days are over. I can see a little of the kitchen from here, too: it has a black-and-white-checked floor, which is something I have always admired.

"I'm sorry," Ginger says, coming out into the hallway, pulling on her coat. "I'd put his leash in a different place—I couldn't find it."

Bones turns, sees the leash in Ginger's hand and becomes excited all over again. "No, no," Ginger says. "We're not going for a walk."

Now his ears perk up and his eyes are like cartoon characters when the money sign comes into them.

"No," Ginger says, laughing.

But she has put Bones's leash on and he has his own ideas. He is dragging her to the door. I mean dragging. Her loafers are planted firm, but she is sliding along like the floor is greased. This is like a comedy show about a happy family.

I look at my father. He is smiling, standing there holding Ginger's suitcase. It seems like we have both almost forgotten what we came here for. But then he takes the leash from Ginger, snaps it smartly and the dog stops pulling. This is the thing about strong people: you can mostly be scared of them but sometimes the way they are makes you feel safe.

Ginger makes the most delicious French toast for my breakfast. It is so fancy, cut into triangles, one lying just a little on top of the other, and it has cinnamon sugar sprinkled on it exactly even. And she squeezed real oranges for my juice! I actually like the can kind better, where things don't clang into your front teeth, but this does taste good and it looks pretty. She folded my napkin, put it neatly under my fork. I guess she thinks this is the Waldorf-Astoria Hotel, moved to Missouri.

"I'm going to Woolworth's with a friend after school today," I tell her. "But I'll be home before dinner."

"Is it Cynthia you're going with?" Ginger is wearing a pink terry-cloth robe, no make-up. One funny thing is she looks better without it. I have never seen that before. Her face is softer, like Doris Day in love.

"No, I'm going with a girl named Taylor," I say. "She's new, too."

Of course, Taylor is new in a way that is the opposite of me. Everyone wants to know Taylor. Everyone is respectful curious. She is aloof, which I guess they like, because they just keep coming back for more. I suppose I like it too. It's like a contest then, who can be the one that she decides to be nice to. What's exciting is that it seems I actually have a chance of winning. I have thought about why. And what I have decided is that the chink that is in Taylor has to do with how much she can feel a thing. She is often moved by what she reads, I know that, I can tell. And she can probably tell that I am, too. When she heard what I said about that poem "Birches" some bored and beautiful part of her said, Well, wait. Maybe here. Maybe there is something here. And maybe there is. I have dressed the best I can, in my navy A-line and a matching sweater. My flip is good. I'm getting used to rollers. I do it for Jimmy but it serves other purposes too. I keep thinking of him as Jimmy even though last time he reminded me again, in a very gentle way, that it is Jim. I think he is wanting some dignity and I am wanting him to be younger. But I will try to remember to call him what he wants until he understands how much love I am putting into "Jimmy."

"Katie?" I hear Ginger say.

"Yeah?"

"Is that all right with you?"

"Is what all right?"

She smiles. "I thought you looked a little far away. What are you thinking about?" The sun catches the edge of the spatula she is holding. There is no more cheerful sight than the sun at breakfast time, touching down on all your ordinary things. It is like Walt Disney himself has sprinkled his dust in your kitchen.

"I don't know, nothing."

She turns back to the pan, flips another piece of French toast. "Well, what I asked you was, is it all right with you if Wayne comes to dinner with us."

"I don't know. I guess so." I'm not sure. My father's not here to ask. I don't know if you just go ahead and have a party when he's gone.

"Would it make you uncomfortable?"

"Me? No."

"All right, then. Plan on dinner at six. Your friend can come too, if you'd like."

"That's okay," I say. One thing I know is that I'll be worn out by four-thirty or five. I'll need a break. When it's new and important, you have to rest in between times. And anyway, even when I like a person there is a weariness that comes. I can be with someone and everything is fine and then all of a sudden it can wash over me like a sickness, that I need the quiet of my own self. I need to unload my head and look at what I've got in there so far. See it. Think what it means. I always need to come back to being alone for awhile. I guess I sort of got used to it when I was younger and now it is mixed in my character like eggs in a cake. Sometimes I wonder, does this mean I'll have to be a nun or something?

After school, Cynthia comes up to me. "Can you come over?" Her eyes are bright.

"Not today," I say. "I'm going to Woolworth's with Taylor Sinn."

"You are?"

"Yes." Now that awful gap part, where she is waiting for me to say, You come too.

I look at my watch. "In fact, I'm late. So I'll talk to you later."

"Okay." Her voice is from when she was a little girl. I walk away and then do the wrong thing, which is turn back and see her standing there, her books all stacked up neat, her hair sticking out wrong on one side, which it always does.

"I'll call you tonight."

She smiles. "Okay!" Well, there. I feel like Clara Barton, nurse.

"Get the patty melt," Taylor says, lighting a cigarette. "That's what I'm getting."

"I don't think so."

"Don't you like them? They're my favorite."

"Yeah, but I don't have that much money. I thought we would just get Cokes."

"Don't worry about it," Taylor says, and then, to the tired waitress, "Two patty melts, extra fries, two Cokes, two apple pies à la mode."

Well, this is the snack *el grande*.

"Á la mode," the waitress says slowly, writing in her pad. Her script is gigantic. I think she is not too bright. But she has the prettiest lips I ever saw. And under her hairnet, beautiful red hair. It's funny how things get scattered around in different ways. Maybe she is a great singer, too.

"Do you like to write?" Taylor asks.

I jerk back to her and me. "I... What do you mean?"

"Do you like to write? You know, stories."

"Oh. Yes. No. Not stories. I like to write...

well, I write some poems sometimes." I don't know if I want to talk about this.

"What are they about?"

Now. A hand to the nest, over the eggs.

"Oh, different things. Do you like to write?"

"I'm working on a novel."

"You are?" Wait, it could be a joke.

She nods, blows smoke out her nose like a dragon. I have never seen a kid do this.

"Yeah, it's about star-crossed lovers. They'll die." She picks a piece of something off her tongue, delicately, flicks it into the ashtray. I have a weird thought to pick it up and keep it.

"Is it long?" I ask.

"I'm up to page seventy-two."

I can't imagine it. "Is it in a notebook?" It might be that we can't help but be friends, as though destiny said, Okay, these two here.

"I type novels," Taylor says. "It's in a box. Hidden. The sex scenes... "

"Oh, I know," I say.

"You want to hear about it?" she asks.

I nod.

And then I don't move again until our order comes. I take a sip of Coke and think steam might come out my ears. That Taylor has a big imagination and she's not afraid to say anything.

When we are through eating, I look at my watch. "We'd better go. You said your sister would be here at four-thirty, right?"

"She's here," Taylor says, pointing out the plate-glass window at a girl walking rapidly toward us. Take Taylor, give her dark hair, make her even more beautiful, and voilà, there is Taylor's sister. "This is Gwen," Taylor says, when she is standing before us.

Gwen holds out her hand and I shake it. I have never done this except with old-fashioned adults. It feels like we're in a new club. Gwen is wearing a brown tweed coat like grown women wear. It is open casually at the throat, and a burnt-orange scarf is there, like a pool of silk.

"Let's go," Taylor says. She takes three dollars from her fat wallet, puts it down on the table and I think, no wonder she didn't care if I don't have any money. She has a lot. Look how much she puts down for just a tip. She probably gets paid plenty for modeling. But then she doesn't take the check up to the register, she puts it inside her math book.

"What are you doing?" I say.

"Let's *go.*" Her face is stiff as a drawing.

And one, two, three, we walk out. We are not even walking fast. We are walking like we are bored. Gwen is not saying "*Tay*lor!" She is rummaging in her purse for her keys.

Huh! I think.

Behind us, the rattle of dishes, the voices of other customers, the distant sound of parakeets huddled miserably in their cages in the corner of the store. I sneak a look behind me and see our waitress on the other side of the room. By the time she gets to our table, we'll be long gone. Wait, she will say. Where's that check, didn't I give them one? Will she panic? Will her stomach hurt? Will she cry?

"Katie," Taylor says.

"Yeah?"

"Don't."

"Okay." I turn back around, walk languidly as summer out to the street.

I sit in the back of Gwen's car, a very clean white Chevrolet with blue seats. I tell them how to get to my house. I am in plain shock. I have just committed a crime. I shiver, then stop. I look out the window, at everybody else.

Ginger is in the kitchen and the smells coming from there could be sold for cash. I realize that I am stuffed as a hog and I am sorry. I don't know why I didn't remember Ginger when I ordered. I was carried on the wave of Taylor. I ate everything she did as though I had to. And she ate everything, period.

"What are you making?" I ask.

Ginger turns around, smiling. "Oh, Katie! Hello!" She wipes her hands on her apron. "Well, let's see. Ham, scalloped potatoes, green beans and tomatoes. Dinner rolls, salad... Oh! And a lemon chess pie."

"Gosh."

"Are you hungry?"

"Sure!"

"We'll eat at six."

Well, I have an hour to get drained.

"You want to do me a favor?" Ginger asks.

"Okay."

"Take the dogs out for a walk? They're in the backyard. They could use some exercise."

That makes three of us.
"Oh, someone called."
Jimmy. "Who?"
"Ed... Edwardo?"
"Oh. Okay." He just wants math help. One thing about being in the dumbest class is I get to be the smartest. It's really not so bad.

I come outside, see Bridgette and Bones lying together like they are engaged. I hope I don't have to call them both at the same time, I'll feel like an idiot.

I put the dogs' leashes on, walk around the side of the house and head down the driveway. There is Greg, out by his mailbox. "Is that yours?" he asks, looking at Bones.

I love that dog's size now for sure. "Yes, he is," I say, casually.

"Oh."

I walk down the street and I know Greg's eyes are on me and I know he is thinking one thing: Sorry. Sorry for all I did.

Well, my life has picked up enough to forgive him. I let my back say it.

Ginger is in the living room with Wayne, watching television. I am in the hall, on the phone with Cynthia. I have my legs up on the wall, which I can't do when my father is home, even if I only have socks on my feet. "Wayne is so boring, I can't believe it," I say. "Plus he has a ducktail! You cannot be a grown fat man and have that! Anyway, it isn't even in style anymore!"

"Eeeuuuwwww," Cynthia says.

"The whole entire time during dinner, he hardly said one thing. Except did I like *Sing Along with Mitch.*"

Cynthia screams so loud I have to pull the phone away from my ear. I am enjoying this conversation. I am sorry to say that sometimes it is just fun to be mean.

"You know what?" Cynthia says.

"What?"

"It's your birthday in a week."

She's right. I'd forgotten. I wonder if my father will be home. He should be in Mexico by tomorrow, if he's not there already. If he comes home pretty soon, he'll be here in time.

"Katie?"

"Yeah?"

"Did you hear me?"

"Yeah. I'd forgotten about my birthday."

"Are you kidding?"

"No."

"I never forget when my birthday comes. I get about six billion presents. Don't you?"

"No." I usually get some clothes, something practical, and then one luxury thing like a book. Although once I did get a charm bracelet.

"Oh. Sorry. Well, I have a present for you. And so does Nona."

I smile. "Really?"

"Yes, but you have to wait till the day. What about your boyfriend, will he give you something?"

"He doesn't know it's my birthday."

"Why not?"

"I don't know. Things are moving kind of slow."

"Well, tell him."

"I don't know. Maybe."

"Tell him! And if you want to move things along, make him jealous."

"How do you know?"

"I've read it everywhere. But it's true, you also see it in every movie. Like Frankie and Annette. What do you *think* works?"

I hear Ginger calling me and I tell Cynthia I have to go. I haven't done a bit of homework yet and it's nine-thirty.

I come into the living room, see Wayne putting his coat on. And his hat which if you can believe it has built-in earmuffs. They are in the up position, trying to hide, but give me a break.

"I enjoyed meeting you, Katie," Wayne says, his voice hearty as Santa Claus.

"Me, too."

"I hope we'll meet again soon!"

"Uh-huh."

"Until then, farewell."

I guess he thinks he's the Lone Ranger.

"Right," I say. "Farewell." Later, when Ginger and I are in our pajamas, I will say, "You know, I think you could do a lot better." I might tell her about Jimmy to give her an idea of what might come if she waits. I might.

I can't believe it, but I am on a real double date. At a drive-in. It is Friday night; I am in the backseat and Taylor is in the front. My date, Mike, does not count as much as Taylor's date, John, because she force-fixed us up, she wouldn't go unless I came. These boys are juniors from St. John's, which is a fancy boys' school. They have dances with Taylor's old school, that's how she met them. Mike has streaked blond hair, blue eyes, a good kind of white sweater, a faint smell of cologne. He has Weejuns on, and no socks. He is too old for me, and he is way too cute, but I am trying. I think he is happy we are at a dark drive-in where he does not have to say to anyone with his eyeballs, *Hey, this was not my idea.* When he first saw me, he did that flash look at his friend, like, Oh boy, later I'm going to kill you. But he is polite and so far it is not too bad.

In the speaker the man is talking about tangy hot pizza that you can buy at the snack bar. And ice-cold Coca-Cola. It makes me hungry.

"So do you like your school?" Mike says.

I have a feeling I could answer "Blue scrambled eggs," and he would just nod.

"Yes," I say. I don't want to get into it.

Previews begin and I can't believe it, Taylor starts making out already. I have heard of this. But there it is.

I can't stop watching them at first. He has his hands in her hair, Cherylanne is exactly right, but then his hand starts moving down. I look out the window. Next to us, a father is yelling at his kids. "Don't," I can hear the wife saying. "Just leave them alone."

Then, just like that, I get full of sadness. I don't know why.

"Do you like Westerns?" Mike asks, and when I turn to answer him, his lips are over mine and his slick tongue is pushing into my mouth. I see an earthworm, churning the dirt.

"Don't!" I pull back, and wipe his warm spit from my face. He is sloppy.

Taylor pulls away from John, looks over at us in the backseat. "What are you doing, Mikey?" she asks, smiling. "Be nice, now."

And then she turns to John. I don't know her. I am deserted here.

"I'm sorry," Mike says, but his arm is still around me, pulling me toward him. I look down, smooth my skirt. When I look up, he is on me again.

I open the car door.

"Where are you going?" Taylor says, laughing a little.

I don't know.

She gets out of the car, comes over to me. "What's wrong?"

"I don't want to be here," I say. In my head, my bed with a book on it, covers folded back. A napkin, two of Ginger's cookies.

Taylor leans into the car. Her skirt is serious tight.

"We need to go to the ladies' room," she says. "We'll be right back."

"Put in your diaphragm," John says, and starts laughing.

Well, what does that mean? Put in a body part.

We are not speaking, Taylor and I. I am setting the pace, and it is fast.

When we get to the bathroom, Taylor takes me by the hand, pulls me into the corner. "What's the matter?" she says. "Don't you think he cute? God! He's *cute*!"

"I know." I notice the concretey smell of urine, see the smeared kiss marks on the wall and the mirror from girls blotting their lipstick.

"So what's the problem?"

"Just because he's cute doesn't mean I want to do that. I don't want to do that."

"Katie."

"What."

"You're in a *drive*-in. What the hell did you expect?"

Well. To watch a movie. Only now I know not to answer with that.

"He should take some time," I say.

"So tell him."

I say nothing, watch a girl in a boy's letter jacket rat her hair up high. She takes a can of hair spray from her gigantic purse, gives it a good squirt, stands back and turns her head this way and that. I am in the exact wrong place.

"This is just for fun," Taylor says. "It's no big deal. It's not like you're going to marry the guy."

I say nothing.

She stands in front of me, bends her knees so we are face to face. “You *need* this,” she says.

“What?”

“Making out! This is the time of your life to start *learn*ing this stuff. Just let him kiss you. It’s not so bad. How do you think you’re going to learn? Sometime it will be really important how you kiss, you don’t want to look like an idiot.”

Maybe she’s right. I don’t know anything about good kissing. What will Jimmy think?

“He won’t *hurt* you. And we won’t do this ever again if you don’t want to, all right?”

She straightens up, sighs loud. The cord between us is stretched dangerous tight.

“All right,” I say. “Fine.”

We go back to the car. I sit with my back to the car next to us so they can’t see me. And then I close my eyes. It isn’t just kissing. He keeps trying to do other stuff. And everywhere on my body that he touches feels like wadded-up Kleenex he is throwing out the window. I am not really here. What’s left behind is only my lonely skeleton, not scary anymore on account of its sadness.

When I get home, I see my father’s car in the driveway. He wasn’t supposed to be back until tomorrow. One reason I got to go out on a date is because Ginger was the one deciding. I hated the car I just got out of, but now I wish I could get back in it. Too late, it is long gone.

I take in a breath, open the door. The dogs

rush up to greet me. Good, Ginger is still here.

He comes out into the living room, stands before me.

"Dad!" I say. "How's Diane?"

"Where were you?"

Behind him, the edge of Ginger. She is holding back, but she is watching. I wonder, did she get in trouble too?

"I had a date. Mike Cassidy is his name, he goes to St. John's. It was a double date, another girl came, Taylor, she's new, too."

"And who told you you could go?"

"Ginger. It's Friday."

"Where did you go that you're coming home this late? Where have you been?"

"I... A drive-in."

His face hardens.

"It's a movie."

"I know exactly what a drive-in is." He steps forward and his arm comes toward my face and I think please, not there, don't do it there. But he is only holding my face in his hand, looking at it. "I know exactly what a drive-in is."

"Frank," Ginger says. *Frank!* But he spins around and now he is on her. Oh, I remember this. Sometimes you are so scared you feel like laughing.

"You don't make decisions like this for my daughter!" He is talking between his teeth the way he does when he gets like this.

She steps back.

But then, when he turns to me again and grabs me, she steps forward one step, then another, then one more until she is beside him, taking his hand off my arm. "Stop it!" she yells. "What's the matter with you!"

Oh, the silence now. The brightness of the lamp by the sofa. The innocence of the magazine on the table.

He looks at her, says nothing. Then he lets go of me, walks away. I hear his bedroom door slam.

A long moment, and then Ginger says, "I'll be here tonight, sleeping on the sofa. Right here in the living room."

"Okay."

I go into my room, close the door. I need to pee, but boy, I won't.

I take off my sweater and skirt, slide into bed with my slip on. I have gone too far. I have been thinking, this is my life. Well, not yet.

I close my eyes, breathe out deep. *What's the matter with you!* she said. Right out loud.

Saturday, we take Ginger out to eat before we take her home. My father is not mad at her. He tells her to get dessert. They have a look pass between them when he drops her off, Bones bouncing behind her. "Thanks," I told her, meaning one thing. "Thanks," my father told her, meaning another.

"You're welcome," she said, to both of us. "I'll see you on Monday."

We talk about Diane for awhile on the way home. He is a little hurt she wouldn't come home. But she was all right. Her body was. I myself am waiting for a letter from her. It could be a very long wait, I know.

Today is my luxury day. One, it is my birthday, and even if you don't get a lot of presents you still can't help being excited, you walk around all day saying your new age to yourself. Two, there is no school on account of the weather. It's only a couple of inches of snow so far, but on the radio they are all worked up. They give the forecast so often any normal person has memorized it. "I *know,*" lots of brains are thinking.

My father will be coming home from work early, he called awhile ago. His job at this place is to recruit young men into the army, talk to the ones who are thinking they'll volunteer about why that's a great idea. I can't imagine how he does it. What can he say? Here's where you'll live!!! Here's what you'll wear!!! I understand they can get their school paid for, maybe that's a reason they sign up. As for me, I'd work somewhere, save up and pay for it myself so it was mine clean. I could tell those young men about the drill sergeants I heard so clearly outside my window where we used to live. Even in cold weather, when the storms were down. That might change their minds. Well, to each his own, my mother used to say, and I suppose she was right.

Since there is no school, I can go to see Jimmy early, stay for hours. I am taking a bath first, and I have rollers in my hair so the steam can help set my curls. I have a Snickers candy bar to eat while I relax in the hot water, which is the heart of the luxury. The chocolate gets soft in just the right way, like it is relaxed, too.

After I have finished eating the candy bar, I rinse my hands, which of course is easy. Then I shave my legs very carefully, nick myself only on the ankle, where there is no chance for any shaver.

When I get out of the tub, I put on my bathrobe, line up the makeup I'll be using in the order that I'll need it. It comes naturally to me now that you wait to get dressed until your makeup is done. I used to do it wrong, put on my good clothes and then take the chance of dropping stuff on them. I like the part when you are finished and you stand back and there is your madeup face all fancy, and you standing in your old bathrobe, which knows everything.

Taylor has taught me how to do eyeliner. You spit on the black cake, swirl around the little paintbrush. Then you VERY CAREFULLY draw a line right above your eyelashes. It is dangerous but worth it. If she could see how I did it today, she'd nod and say, "Yeah." Plus she gave me some Pan-Cake makeup, the stick kind, for my face. This is not working out so well. I just look greasy. I take some toilet paper, pat at it, but no, it still looks awful. I'm not sure what I've done wrong.

"Katie?"

It's Ginger at the door.

"Are you almost done in there?"

No. "Yeah."

"Okay. Let me know."

I hear her walk away, hear the vacuum go on. But she'll be back soon—polite, but in need. I can never get enough time in here. Cynthia has two bathrooms and that is exactly what we need. Now I will have to move to my bedroom and that will break the spell and nothing will come out right.

I rub off the pan stick. I'll just use some eyeliner and some lipstick. Maybe white, which is the latest. I have some of that from Taylor, too. She is the generous kind, who, if you say, oh that's nice, she throws it at you, says, keep it. I have never seen a kid who seems not to care about so much.

"I'm out," I yell to Ginger, then go into my room. I'm wearing a red sweatshirt that looks good on me, and one necklace, and that is it for jewelry. I'll have to wear my galoshes, but they can come off. I inspect my socks for holes. Not a one.

"King me," Jimmy says.

"Man oh man," I say. "You're hot today."

"You're not concentrating," Jimmy says.

"I am too." Not on checkers, of course.

Jimmy leans back in his chair, stretches, looks at his watch. "Wow, one o'clock!" I am flattered that so much time has gone by unbeknownst to him.

"Are you hungry?" he asks.

"No. Well. Some."

"Want some lunch?"

"I don't know." Eating in front of him is not something I'm quite ready for. Sounds happen.

He opens his sack lunch, pulls out a fat sandwich wrapped in waxed paper. "I'll give you half," he says.

"No," I say. "That's okay. I have to go soon."

"Stay," he says. "Eat some of this. It's a big sandwich, I made it too big." *He* made it! What oh what does his wife do, lie around in blue negligees reading articles in the movie magazines about Charlton Heston?

I take half the sandwich. It's ham and cheese. Find me one man who doesn't like that. That is the man's sandwich, and chicken salad is the woman's.

It's a good thing I came to see Jimmy today, he would have been bored silly. The weather is keeping the cars off the road. It turned out to be a great storm, worse than they thought. Big fat flakes are coming down fast now. It looks like a paper factory blew up. But also it's romantic. I wish I didn't live so close. Then I could have the chance of being stranded here with him. Night would fall. I would lie on the floor close to him and I wouldn't see him, I would only hear him breathing. One thing would lead to the other until we were kissing. He might say my name in my ear. Which maybe I *should* change to Katherine.

"Katie?"

I look up.

He laughs. "I swear, I never saw such a daydreamer. What are you always thinking about?"

I feel myself flushing, a disaster. "Nothing," I say, and then, "Today is my birthday."

His mouth opens in surprise, he leans back in his chair. It matters to him.

"Why didn't you tell me?"

I shrug.

"So you're fifteen now!"

Oh. Oh, yes, that's right. I'm so glad he said that before I leaked out thirteen. I nod.

"Well, happy birthday, Katie!"

"Thank you."

"I feel badly that I don't have a present for you."

"Well. We're just new. It's okay. It's fun to be here, that's a present."

"No." He looks around the room, frowning. "Want a spark plug?"

I smile. He has a smart sense of humor.

"Wait, I do have something." He reaches in his pocket, pulls out a flat stone, puts it in my hand. It's a beautiful gray-green color, speckled, smooth as an egg.

I look up at him.

"It's lucky," he says. "Honest."

"How come?"

"It just is. And it's... Well, it's kind of soothing. If I feel nervous about something, I rub it. I don't know, it helps." He shrugs. I think he's starting to regret offering it to me.

"I really like it," I say, "but I don't want to take it."

"Oh no," he says. "Take it. I'd like for you to have it." He puts it in my hand.

I hear the low buzz of the fluorescent light above us. This could be the time when I should say something, make things move along. In my throat is the whole sentence, "I think I love you."

I look up at him and in his face is only a kind affection. Oh, he is twenty-three, he is twenty-three and I am stupid thirteen. His mother should have waited awhile to have him. I guess I will never get to meet his mother. I look down at the stone, close my hand around it. This is what I have.

"I had a date Friday night," I tell him. *Make him* jeal*ous,* I hear Cynthia saying.

"Hey! Good for you!"

Cynthia is an imbecile.

"I have to go," I say, standing. I didn't know love could take your stomach up in its hands and squeeze it until it hurt.

Jimmy stands too. "Now?"

Hope. "Well..." Ask me to stay. Say, Oh, Katie...

"I'm sorry, it's okay. It was nice of you to stay so long. I'd have been pretty bored, otherwise."

"You have your books," I say. I'd seen the pile on his desk.

He looks at them. "Yeah, that's right. I do like to read."

"What have you got?"

"One is a mystery," he says. "And one is a biography, about Lincoln. The other is called

The Winter of Our Discontent. Do you like John Steinbeck?"

I nod. He reads! Us in bed at night, both of our lamps on, both of us with books. "Listen to this," I'd say, and he would say, "Nice. But listen to this." His wrists, out a ways from his pajama sleeves.

He grins, and I nearly throw up with longing.

"You're surprised that I read anything but auto mechanics, right?"

"No." Kind of.

"Know what I wanted to do, Katie?"

"What?"

"Be a writer."

Well, I am going home to flat die.

"Why didn't you?"

"Oh, you know. You get a family, you have to support them."

"I'm sorry."

"No, it's... fine. It's a little hard, now, that's all. But it's fine."

"I wish..." I say. I don't know what I wish. I wish too much.

"What?" he says, and in his face is a yearning, too.

Unless I'm wrong.

"I don't know. I wish you could have whatever you wanted. All that you want." My voice has gotten thick.

He smiles at me and it is a new kind of look, a careful one mixed with a new knowledge. "Well. I wish that for you too, Katie."

"Okay." Oh, I don't even know what we're

talking about. It is too full in me. I can't even swallow against it. I start for the door.

"So I'll see you soon, okay?"

I turn back, smile, nod. There it is, my birthday gift supreme.

I feel sort of happy on the way home. I can't wait to lie down and think, what was that? What was the whole, real conversation? Maybe things *are* moving along! If only that could be true, I would do so many good things to pay for it.

Dear Katie,

Well you will not believe the sentence you are going to read next. I am coming to visit you!!!! That is if it is all right with your father, of course. My mother told me the other day that I can come on the train over Christmas vacation and spend three days.

You may wonder why.

Well, here is the whole story. I have broken up with Todd. It was not my fault or Eric's, who is that basketball boy I told you about. These things just happen when you are young, as my mother agrees. But Todd! He was all hurt and started rumors about me like you would not believe, such as I did things with him that I did not. *Which I already told you, how I had decided on things in my head long before my body was put to the test. I don't think I have to remind you about the morals I hold near and dear, plus once you are used merchandise there go all your plans for other things in your life. Anyway he was telling everyone these vile lies and I don't know what is wrong with them, half the kids believed them and also ERIC believed it. There I soon was, alone. And with people talking. And no boys calling me except greasers. I warn you, Katie, this happened so fast and vicious. Well I was bent by grief into a shell of my former self. I thought I might have to enter the loony bin. But then thank God my mother said, Well, would it help you to just get away a little, why don't you visit Katie? And I think it would help to have a change of scenery, plus I could see your boyfriend who I hope still is your boyfriend although from what I have been going through nothing would surprise me.*

Anyway, so write me back (or call me!!!!!) and let me know is it okay? I could come the weekend of the 16th. Naturally I would have to come home for the main part of the holidays. But by then I know that our friendship could help me.

I have to say that I never thought this could happen to me and I would advise you in your life to be ever watchful.

Love,

Cherylanne

P.S. How come you hardly write anymore?

It is a Saturday morning. My father has just come back from the grocery store. I start unloading the bags. Good, I see he bought some Lay's potato chips and they are exactly right, you cannot eat just one. Plus Hawaiian Punch, which shows he is in a good mood. Everybody wants to buy it because they get to say, "Hey, want a Hawaiian punch?"

"I got a letter from Cherylanne," I say. "She wants to know if she can come and visit here."

He pulls out a package of sardines. He eats those things. On soda crackers.

"December 19th, for a few days. She'd come on the train."

He stops pulling out groceries, thinks a little. "I suppose that's all right."

"So I'll tell her yes?"

"Yeah."

"Can I call her?"

He looks at me.

"Or I could write."

"Why don't you do that."

I finish putting away groceries, go back into my room. I am not so excited. I used to be under Cherylanne, but I just don't think I am anymore.

"Thirteen!" Nona says. She is sitting up today in a chair by her bed, her feet on a hassock, a plaid blanket over her lap.

"Right. Thirteen."

"That's-a big!"

"I guess."

"Little *woman.*" Nona cackles softly, and I get a little nervous. Cynthia says if Nona laughs hard, she wets her pants. She says Nona has underwear that is much too big for her now, but she won't part with them. She wears safety pins to keep them up. "They're *huge,*" Cynthia said. "Like flags or something."

"It's-a time for love, no?" Nona says, in her low, secret voice.

This startles me. What does she know? What has Cynthia told her?

"I don't know," I say. "I guess."

"I'm-a give you something," Nona says, and from under her blanket she pulls out a battered black book. It looks like a diary. She opens it, reads a little, smiles, closes it again. Then she hands it to me.

"You're giving this to me?"

"Happy birthday to you."

"But... This is your diary, isn't it?"

"It's-a the book from *love.*"

I open to the first page. It's in Italian. "I can't read it, Nona."

She shrugs. "What's the difference? It's-a to *feel.*"

"Oh! Well. Thank you." I am shy grateful. And I think I do feel something, already.

Nona leans forward. "I had-a love."

I nod.

"You know how it was? It was like-a trees. Oak and elm." Her voice has been soft, like it was lost in memory, but now she stares at me, her eyes narrowed, and she makes a fist and pounds the side of her chair. "The roots, they bound-a together, but the trees, they are free. You know what it's-a mean?"

I nod, but I'm not sure. Cynthia told me that when her grandfather died, he'd been in the garden picking tomatoes. Nona looked through the window, saw him lying down and ran out and kicked him. She thought he was sleeping. She was yelling at him for being lazy and then when he didn't move, she knelt down and saw. She held him in her arms, kept his straw hat on his head, rocked him for hours. And then she went to her room and didn't come out except for the funeral. This went on for months. And then came the day when she came into the kitchen and put her apron back on. Fiercer.

"You gotta have you tree. He's-a gotta his. No?"

"Yes." I rub my hand gently over the cover of the diary. It's old leather, softened and nearly touching back, the way that old leather will. I actually like it better than what Cynthia gave me, which is a best-friends necklace. I got one half of a heart, she got the other. Now I will have to wear it every day or she will say, all hurt, "What's wrong?"

"You gotta boyfriend?" Nona asks. Her eyes are watery, pleading.

"Yes," I say softly.

"Ha!" she says. "I'm-a think right!"

In bed that night, I turn the thin pages of Nona's diary. I like that I can't read it. This way, the story will change and change. I find places where she underlined, places where it looks like tears fell on the page. The diary whispers and whispers, sighs and sighs, and then, on one page, yells out loud. It's huge writing, just three words but they are happy, you can tell, the writing is happy. Cynthia said Nona gave the diary to me so Mrs. O'Connell would never read it. She said Nona's been giving lots of things away lately. She gave Cynthia all her jewelry, wrapped in a few of her man-sized handkerchiefs. We sat on Cynthia's floor and took it out and put it all on. It was a lot. We put rings on our toes, necklaces on our ankles, draped bracelets from our ears. There was so much, we had to improvise. It was pretty amazing fun. We felt like forgiven thieves.

I have outdone myself on the macaroni and cheese, if I do say so myself. Miss Woods said put it under the broiler for just a second and you have a crust all will admire. And she is right.

Not that my father is admiring it. He is just eating as though he is reading the newspaper, but there is no newspaper.

"What do you think of Ginger?" he asks.

"Pardon?"

"I said, what do you think of Ginger?"

"I think she's great!" Please don't fire her, I'm thinking. And then I think, Oh.

"Why?" I say.

He looks at me, tongues off a tooth, shakes his head. "No reason. Just wondering."

"Don't you like her?" Inside I get a dangerous feeling, like something growing bigger and bigger in there.

"Yeah. I do like her. She does a fine job and... Yeah."

"Yeah," I say. This conversation sounds like idiots. The words we are saying, that sounds like idiots. The words we are meaning scare me to death. I'd forgotten about this, how he might find someone else. I just don't know if it's all right. The pain of missing my mother has been a dull and distant thing. Not anymore.

* * *

"What do you think of my father?" I ask Ginger. It is Monday, and she's made herself a cup of tea to have before she goes home. She made me Jell-O with peaches and I put mayonnaise on top of it like frosting, which I wouldn't let just anyone see.

She looks at me, smiles. "Well."

"No, for real," I say.

"Okay." Her face grows serious. We are eyeball to eyeball. Woman to woman. I straighten in my seat. "I like him quite a bit, Katie. I think I'm in love with him."

"What about Wayne?"

"Well... Wayne. You know, I like Wayne. But he's..." She puts down her cup. "I have always liked a little danger in a man, Katie. That's the truth. I can't tell you why, or that it's a good thing. But it's the truth. I like a kind of... well, yes, that's it, I like a kind of *dan*ger."

"Well, that is one thing *he* is."

"Yes, I know. But you know, your father has a great capacity for tenderness. He feels things, Katie."

I look down at my Jell-O. I know he does. And now I see I am not the only one who knows. It is a relief and a sorrow.

We have come to this inside junction. I could get kind of mean now, let her know I'm going to fight this. But I'm tired. I think I'm ready. And last night, late, in those velvet hours when sleep is one-half there and the truth comes, I asked my mother, Was this all right? What she told me more or less is that there is room in life for more than we imagine.

"He likes that dress you wore the other day," I say.

"The blue one?"

"Yes."

"Oh," she says, and I think she is starting to blush a little. "Well, thank you."

"You're welcome."

My mother said directly to me it was all right, but I'll tell you, a hurt has come in me like a Mack truck. Nothing against Ginger, really.

"I have to do my homework," I say, around the sideways ache in my throat.

"Okay." She knows I'm lying clean through.

I start to put my dishes in the sink and she says, "Leave it, honey. I'll do everything."

"All right," I say. I know that, too.

It is Saturday afternoon, and I am shopping with Taylor. First we went to Steinbeck's and I got to watch her walk around in front of people, wearing outfits. She knows how to do all the model things: walk out so sauntering, turn in a pretty circle, walk back, haughty on her long legs. She was the prettiest one, no contest. Her sister wasn't there, they alternate weeks.

Then we went out to lunch at a little restaurant with lace curtains and the same thing happened, Taylor left a tip and pocketed the bill. I started to say something but she said, "It's no big deal. Don't worry about it. They figure this in. As long as you leave a tip, it doesn't hurt anyone."

"What happens if we get caught?" I asked, on the way out. Taylor acted like I hadn't said a word until we got about a block away. Then she said, "Don't ever say that, about getting caught."

I got a terrible sinking feeling then, like I just wanted to go home. We are too different. But there is something about Taylor, like the pull of a magnet. She knows how to change people's moods, even when they don't want them to be changed. I think she is the kind people say "She could charm the devil" about. I can see it, the devil putting down his pitchfork, saying, "Oh, all *right.*"

Now we are in the dressing room of a fancy store and Taylor is trying on clothes. I didn't see anything I wanted to try, so I'm just watching. The women who work here make me nervous. They act like they're doing you a favor being here, they could be oh so many other better places. They are all pretty but fading, when they look down, you can see their skin is loose like an elephant. There are scarves and gold jewelry in cases, dresses lined up with plenty of space between them, all on fancy hangers. The dressing rooms have real doors, gold hooks to hang things on, pretty little benches inside in case you get tired from snapping and zipping.

Taylor has on a beautiful blue skirt and sweater. They go together. "That's nice," I say. Underneath, she has on a bra that is the same exact flowered material as her underpants. Her underwear is an outfit, too. Every day.

"Yeah, it *is* nice," she says, turning to inspect how she looks from behind. She is chewing gum, cracking it loud. Those women didn't mind anything about Taylor. They took her seriously, like she comes in every day and says charge it to one million dollars, even though she has never been in here before. Me, they knew about. Taylor says you have to come into these stores looking like a million bucks, then the old bags leave you alone. "Uh-huh," I said, like this was a possibility for me.

She pulls off the sweater, steps out of the skirt, folds them both up small.

"Are you going to buy them?" I ask.

"Yeah, they're on special."

"How much?" One sweater I'd looked at had a price tag of $88. I'd put it back gently and then put my hands in my pockets.

"Free."

I watch as she crouches down and stuffs the outfit in her purse.

Now, this is too much.

"I'm going," I say. "I'll wait for you outside."

She looks up at me, some of her famous hair over one eye.

"You're going to get in trouble, Taylor."

She looks around the dressing room. "You see how many clothes I brought in here?"

"Yes."

"You think they're going to notice one outfit gone?"

"I don't know."

"They won't. Believe me."

"Well, I'm just going."

"Fine." She doesn't look up.

I walk on the thick, pale blue carpet to the door. Then I get nervous. If I just stand there, I may look like I'm a get-away person. They may suspect her. One saleslady, her half-glasses perched meanly on her nose, is watching me like a vulture. I smile, go over to the dresses.

"Something I can help you with?" she asks from across the room, which shows just how sincere she is.

"I'm just looking," I say and study the

polka-dot dress in front of me. Even though it's navy blue and white, the belt is red.

Taylor comes out of the dressing room, walks up to the counter, her wallet out. She is carrying a black belt with a silver buckle.

"That's all?" the woman behind the counter says, but it is a nice voice, almost like a flirty sound.

"For today," Taylor says, and looks her right in the eye, bored and tired-kind, like she is saying, You are one lucky lady to get to help me, now get on with it.

The women rings the belt up—fifty dollars!—and Taylor pays. And then she heads toward me. I have a sudden image of a cane going around her neck, yanking her back, and a policeman all dressed in blue with a big star on his chest taking my arm and saying, "You too, little lady." This doesn't happen, of course. Nothing does.

Next we go into a department store, to the lingerie department. Taylor brings handfuls of things into the dressing room, puts three bras and three pair of panties on under her clothes, and walks out. I don't know why I'm watching this. Something has been sucked out of me and I am walking around on hollow legs.

I am lying in bed that night, thinking about how it would feel to have stolen underwear in my drawer. I'll bet it feels kind of exciting every time you put it on. It would never be ordinary underwear. "Hey," it would be saying all the time. "Remember?"

I hear the phone ring, hear my father answer it. Then he comes into my room. "Phone call. What are they doing calling so late?" He walks away. It's a good thing something he likes is on television.

I come into the hall, pick up the phone, say hello.

"What, are you sleeping?" Taylor says.

"No. I was in bed, though."

"Listen, I wanted to tell you I'm sorry."

"About what?"

"You know."

"Well."

"It made you sort of scared, right?"

"No." Sometimes you don't like someone to come right out and say the thing.

"Yes, it did. I could tell. We won't do that together anymore."

"Okay."

"We'll do other things."

Crime? I think.

"I'll take you to hear some good music or something next weekend. I'll get you a date."

I look carefully at the phone dial. There's dust in there.

"Katie?"

"Yeah?"

"You won't have to do anything."

"I know."

But I didn't.

"I'm not sure," I hear myself say. "I might not be able to."

"Fine. Suit yourself."

She hangs up.

Well, now she's mad. I might have lost this. And then I will just have Cynthia. I call her back, and she answers on the first ring.

"Okay," I say.

I go back to bed, close my eyes, but they feel they are stark open. Something once so sure in me is getting all mixed up. Many things can be true, all at the same time. I don't know how you can be expected to be a person and keep up, it is just too complex. I saw the structure of an atom once and I thought, well, if that is only an *atom,* just think what all is in the sack of a whole human being. I can see now it was exactly the right thing to think. But what do I do about it?

"Sugar cookie?" Father Compton asks.

"No thank you."

"Well, would you mind if..."

"Oh no! No, you go right ahead."

He sits back in his chair, takes a good-sized bite, says around it, "So!" Little crumbs fly out and he gets embarrassed, but I make my face like, Oh it's fine, I didn't see a thing.

We are in his office and I have a whole half hour if I want, which is so generous on his part, since I told him today we have no intention of joining, not my father or me. I thought I should make it clear. Father Compton said that was fine, that was fine, but he was a little disappointed, plus also I think he believes he could get me eventually anyway.

I came because I trust him and he is not a friend or a relative. I didn't plan what to say,

I thought it would just come out when I sat here, but I was wrong. I don't exactly know how to start.

"How have you been?" he asks, after a swallow of coffee, which always smells so good but then when you taste it you get a bitter surprise. And you always want to taste it again because how could your nose be so wrong? but it is.

"I've been fine," I say. And then, "I have some trouble. I mean, I've been..."

He waits.

I wait.

"I have a friend who has been stealing," I say, finally.

"Uh-huh."

Well, he is not even surprised. He takes another bite of cookie!

"It was kind of a shock to me."

"Yes, well, it's not uncommon, Katie. People your age are often tempted to steal things." He looks deep and significantly at me.

"It's not me I'm talking about," I say quickly.

"Uh-huh."

"Really!"

"All right."

Well, this is going down the wrong path.

"If it were me, I would say so."

Nothing.

"I have a friend, Taylor is her name, she's the one."

"I see. And what has she stolen?"

"Well, she never pays for meals out. And she stole a whole outfit last week, put it in her purse, and it cost over one hundred and fifty dollars."

Well. Now he is interested. I know what he was thinking. He was thinking, oh, gum, candy. Maybe a lipstick or two. But now he is sitting up straight and official. Everybody gets interested in Taylor, one way or another.

The ice on the pond is good today—light blue smooth, very little snow blown over it. Jimmy will watch me when he can, I know it, that's our way. Then I'll come in the station, and we'll talk. Step by step, is what I need to do. Soon it will be Christmas vacation and then I'll have more time. It is my personal goal that by day five, I'm going to say, "Jimmy, do you have any kind of feeling for me?" I can do it if I pick the right time, and I know how to pick the right time. It will be after we talk about older men and younger women. I have an article from the paper to get us going. It's about how a sixty-five-year-old married a forty-year-old, which is worse than us. The man is a millionaire, of course, which is what these things usually are. But this is my twist: I will say, It seems to me to be possible that a younger woman would love an older man for his own self, too.

I skate a good half hour, although it is hard to keep from cutting it short when I know where I'm going when I'm through. But it's good not to be so obvious, to act like, well, I would be here anyway.

I am up to the station, about ready to open the door when I look through the glass and what slams into my eyes but the sight of Jimmy kissing someone. His arms are tight around her waist which is so small and his eyes are closed like he is praying. I breathe out, step back. I hate the white my breath has left in the air.

I am walking away when the door opens. I hear the little bell and then I hear Jimmy say, "Katie!"

I turn around. "It's okay," I say.

"No, come here! There's someone I want you to meet."

Oh my God. It's his wife. I smile, head back toward him. I have to do this, even though the word WIFE is walking out toward me, tall as a wall. Everything I ever thought about him and me is the stupidest thing.

"No," Cherylanne says, "you must not give up now. This is only the challenge part. No woman ever got a good man without a challenge. Otherwise you wake up one day and you are bored. This way, you have a deep contentment all your life."

It is late at night, and we are still talking. Cherylanne arrived at 3:47, we came home, shut my bedroom door, and here is where we have been since except for dinner and the bathroom. If you think you don't care so much for someone anymore, just see them. So many things have come back, it feels like I'm standing under a shower of Cherylanne and me. I am so happy to be lying here beside her on my bed, it's like the old days, including that she has the better pillow. Even though she said she has been emotionally battered and bruised she is willing to help me, to tell me all I have to do. "I am still strong on the advice front," she said. "Just tell me everything. Don't leave anything out. I must know the whole truth just like when you go to the judge. And then I can help you."

And she has helped me. For example, when I told her about Jimmy kissing his wife and how it hurt so bad like a fist in my heart she said, "How do you know it was *him* kissing *her?* How do you know she didn't walk in and smack one on him and he was suffering? Why else would he want you to come in?"

That made me feel so much better. It could be true! The more I thought about it, the more I realized he didn't act like he ever wanted me to leave. And his wife was pretty, with her dark curly hair, but she was mean, I could tell it a mile away. She smiled at me with her lips pressed together and I slunk home, but now I see I could have looked straight at her like, Yup, that's right, you'd better go home and think how to keep your man. I feel inspired, now. The battle has just begun.

"Have you brought him food?" Cherylanne yawns.

"No."

"Well, Katie."

"What?"

"You have really overlooked the basics."

"He gave me some food."

"Well, that is pure backward."

I think about his sandwich, the tenderness of our sharing. I can make quite a few things now. I can make an angel cake that gets some of its insides plucked out and then you put in strawberries and whipped cream instead. My mother always liked that cake. It was fancy. I could bring it on a plate and he would say, Wow, you made this? Sure, I would say, and I would tell him that also I could make a whole dinner to go with it.

"What else?" I ask Cherylanne. I hope I don't forget what she says. Maybe I should write it down.

"Well, try using some big words. He'll think you're more mature."

"Like what?"

Quiet.

Then she says, "Well, it depends on the situation. And on what kind of man he is, which of course I don't know."

"I'll take you to meet him."

"And will I meet Taylor, too?"

"Sure."

"Oh, good."

Everybody likes outlaws. Everybody wants to look at them, like they are in the zoo.

Well, this was the mistake of the century. Taylor and Cherylanne are not a good mix and I say this in the extreme. So far they have eyeballed each other and said little minced words that only mean *"I could not care less about you, girl."* It was instant hate. I never saw anything like it. Later I will hear an earful from both of them. For now, I am giving it five more minutes and then saying we have to go. I'd thought we could have a conference on Jimmy. I'd thought we could try on clothes and makeup. Well, that is as far away from us sitting here in the deep freeze of Taylor's room as Pluto is from earth. If that is the last planet, that is what I mean. Whoa, my brain is saying, were you wrong. And in a high wounded tone I hear both their brains saying back to me, That's *right.* Imagine a brain with its arms crossed, stubborn. That is them. This is the most severe case of bad first impressions I hope to ever see. I would say it will be the only impression, too.

"It is just chemical, and you can't fight that," Cherylanne tells me that night after dinner. Her face is different. One eyebrow is higher than the other, and her nose is pinched.

"I don't know what happened," I say. "I thought you'd like her."

"Well, I'll tell you what, I hope I never again see anyone with her nose so high in the air as Miss la-de-dah Taylor Sinn. Good Lord, if it rains, that girl will drown."

I say nothing.

Cherylanne keeps going. "Like I care that she's a model! Like I care that she thinks she is the best-looking thing since Rosalind Russell!"

"Who's that?"

"Just never mind, Katie, that's not the point we're on." She looks at her nails. I see. She doesn't know who Rosalind Russell is either. Sometimes she just likes to use certain names she's heard. FDR, she said once, and she didn't even know what the initials were for.

She didn't even know it was a person! I think she got it mixed up with FYI. She does know Einstein, which she uses quite a bit.

In my head is the quiet thought that Cherylanne has at last met someone much better-looking than she is. And that that's all this is. Cherylanne started everything. But I'm not mad, I actually feel tender for her. She is just a visitor and things are not going well for her at home.

"So what did you think of Jimmy?" I say. I will give her the relief of another subject, even though I know exactly what she thought of him. She practically needed to put her eyeballs on a leash.

"Oh, my God," she says, flopping back against the pillow. "Katie, if you could win him, you would be the luckiest woman alive."

"I know. Plus he's nice."

"Oh! Nice! He is... he is..."

"I know," I say.

"He cannot be in love with his wife and still be the way he is with you."

"You think?"

"I *know.*" She might know. Or she might be trying to say things that I will like on account of Taylor. "I saw how he stared at you when you weren't looking."

I look at her quick.

"Really, I swear!"

Well, all right. Fine.

"Want some more peach crisp?" I ask. Celebrate.

"Okay." She stands up, straightens her

sweater and checks her face even though we are only going to the kitchen. “You know, Katie,” she says to her mirror self, “you’re lucky to have such a good cook as Ginger. Eating well is half the battle for a flawless complexion.” And then, before we leave my bedroom, she takes me by the arm. “Are she and your father—”

“Yes,” I say, “I’ll tell you later.” We head out to the kitchen. We’ll get some dessert and then come back and talk about Ginger. We have so much to do before she leaves. We haven’t even started on her troubles yet. I don’t believe I’ve moved up to where I can give her advice, but I will listen as long as she wants because of all she told me about Jimmy.

The day after Cherylanne leaves, we are eating dinner when my father says, "Just who is this Taylor person?"

I swallow my mouthful of food, grown suddenly larger.

"Taylor Sinn?"

"Yeah. Her."

"Well, she's... you know, that new girl at school." Who said what, I'm thinking. Ginger? Cherylanne?

"You've been spending a lot of time with her."

"Yeah, I guess so."

"What do you do with her?"

Who said what?

"I don't know. Mostly just shopping and stuff like that."

"Why doesn't she ever come here?"

"I don't know."

"I'd like to meet her."

"All right."

"She's the one you went to the drive-in with, right?"

"Right."

"Well, I want to meet her."

"Okay."

Silence. And then he says, "Ginger and I are going to be going out to dinner tomorrow night. You all right with that?"

"Yes."

I think what it is, is he's trying to be fair.

Lying in bed that night, I think of when I asked my mother about how she met my father. She blushed, telling me. It was at an ice-cream parlor. They were each sitting in booths, across from each other, each of them with other people, dates. Julian was her date's name, Susan was his. And the next day, she and my father each came back at the same time, alone. "How'd you know he'd be there?" I asked.

"I don't know," she answered, smiling. "But you'll know, too, when it's your time."

Oh, where is she? A stubborn part of me had thought this might be over sometime. But she is staying gone and staying gone and staying gone. She is not in the grave, though. No, she isn't. I have her out of the grave. And right now I put her in a yellow flowered dress, a pale yellow apron over it. It has ruffles and the ruffles are eyelet. I don't know if there is such a thing, really. But now there is, and I am sitting at the kitchen table watching her shape the piecrust edges into their stand-up design. She is concentrating so hard her tongue sticks out a little. This really used to happen. Once I laughed and she said, What are you laughing about? and I told her her tongue was sticking out and she said, "It was not!" Well, there are things you can't see about yourself. I loved that she stuck her tongue out that way. It was cute, like when a kitten is done washing and his hair sticks up on top of his head. I never said anything about her doing that again. I wish I could have. I wish I could have gone through my long list of all the things I loved about her before she died. Right in front of her. I don't believe my memory would have failed me one bit, even if I was crying the whole time, saying those things. Saying all those things that made her her.

After English, I tell Taylor my father wants to meet her.

She stands looking at me, saying nothing.

"Can you?" I say, finally.

"Can I what?"

"Can you meet him?"

"What for?"

"He's just curious. He knows I like you."

She nods, stares after a boy who just passed in the hall. He's a senior. I believe she's thinking, Hmmm, do I want to bother?

"What's he like?" she asks.

I turn, see the boy disappearing around the corner. "I don't know. He's a senior." Someday I'll be a senior with my ring that lets me butt up in the lunch line.

"No, your father."

"Well, he's... you know, I told you."

"What's he look like?"

Well. He looks like my father.

"He's tall. Big."

"Fat?"

"No. Just big. He has blue eyes. Black hair. But it's in a crew cut."

She shrugs. "I'll come over for dinner. I want you to help me do my sonnet anyway."

Mrs. Brady has given us all that assignment, to write a sonnet, which is kind of like a poem wearing high heels. It's because we've been reading Shakespeare's sonnets. Everybody groaned but me. I felt a blip of secret happiness. It will be a challenge, but I am grateful to try it. Shakespeare! I always wanted to say his name in casual conversation. Someday I will have a house with a fireplace and I will have all the things he wrote in a big leather book nearby, gold print on a red cover. You have to puzzle him out, Shakespeare, but it's worth it. Just sit down by the fire in your velvet robe and take your time. Let the clock be ticking a little bit loud, the pendulum flashing on the upstroke from the angle of the sun. Say the words out loud to yourself, taste them like they are food. Which they are. Have tea nearby in a silver pot, the spout as graceful as a swan's neck. Your cup should be china, so thin light can push through it. This to me beats lying on the floor chewing bubble gum and reading *Archie and Veronica,* which is what most kids my age like. Although Shakespeare is dead, I hope he knows what an honor it is to be him.

I want nice paper to write my sonnet on, too. I wish it could be thick and cream colored, which I read about in a story and it made me want to write on that too. The words "heart" and "glass" have come to me. It's enough to start with. It excites me, like the way you feel walking up on a butterfly. *Stay,* you're thinking. You reach out, moving so slow when you're dying to just crash forward.

I don't think Taylor really needs any help. She makes *A*s in everything without even trying, even in chemistry, which usually you have to be a sophomore to take. I've never known her to study. "It's all obvious," she said, when I asked her how she could do that. "It's easy." We were in her room, each of us lying on a twin bed.

"Maybe you need a harder school," I said.

She smiled. "I tried that."

"How come you left that school, anyway?"

"How come you ask so many questions?"

I stayed still for a minute, thinking, then raised up on one arm. "Did you get kicked out?"

She got up, walked over to her dresser, started combing her hair. "I hated that school. It was a bunch of girls." She turned around. "You ever hear of Howlin' Wolf?"

"No."

"He's a blues singer."

"He is?"

She held up a record album featuring a huge black man, sweating. "This is him, right here." She stared at it, then handed me the album. "He's my father."

"Right."

"Really!"

I looked up at her. Her eyes were wide open and staring straight at me, full of the wound of not being believed. Well, I have never met her father. Her parents are separated, and he never comes around. Probably because her mother is so strange. She's always in a hurry; she's always saying, "Oh Jesus, oh Jesus, I'm eons late." Plus she lived in Greenwich Village which is that place in New York City. She used to be a great beauty, you can tell, but it is all being erased. She's an artist, she has a studio out in the garage and does gigantic paintings that you don't know what are. She forgets important things, like to make dinner. She's really different from any other mother I've ever seen. But still. "That is not your father," I told Taylor.

She laughed.

She can be like that, sort of weird. But then she will do something that shows off a talent of hers and you can't help it, you want so bad to be her friend. Once she read a whole play to me, acted out all the parts and she was so good. I couldn't believe it was really Taylor. It was a Tennessee Williams play, *Summer and Smoke.* Taylor was not really there. She was replaced by each character she read. She is like a sparkler you cannot stop watching and want to touch so badly. Her sister is only beautiful. She doesn't have this sharp genius of Taylor. I think that's what it is, she is a genius. And you have to cut a genius some slack sometimes. That's how they are. I ended up just combing Taylor's hair that day, lifting a section now and then to feel the silky weight in my hands.

Sometimes I would get down next to her face and put her hair on me to see how I would look as a fabulous blond. Sometimes she let me do that.

It is such an odd thing to have a Christmas with only two people. It might be worse than being alone. My father and I opened our few presents, then sat for awhile by the tree, each of us thinking that's what the other one wanted to do, I guess. My father gave me twenty dollars to buy him something and I just got him a wallet and a duck call. He never will use that duck call. It was one of those things, I was feeling desperate and the guy selling the duck calls honked it and I thought, Isn't that cute! Maybe my father will think that's *funny!* and I bought it. But he just said all serious, Well, thank you, Katie and then he laid it carefully back in the box. I got knee socks, pajamas, a book of poems by Americans and a stuffed animal, a cat wearing a dress. She's cute, but really I am too old, she'll have to live in my closet. The best gift was Intimate perfume and dusting powder. So I guess Ginger helped a bit with shopping. I kept wishing someone else was there so I could have another face to look at, a triangle of possibility instead of just a deadly straight line.

After awhile we went out for Chinese food, and my father left a big Christmas tip and the waiter nodded and nodded and said "Happy Christmas, Happy Christmas" about three hundred times. We went for a little walk afterward and my father's hands were deep in his pockets and his head was hanging low. I didn't even try. I just walked beside him and kept looking at the stars, trying to think which one was the Star of Bethlehem, which I think is one of the prettiest phrases I've ever heard, Star of Bethlehem. I thought, what if I were a Wise Man, what would the message be now? Maybe just God saying, Well, they are wrong about me. I did once make a terrible mistake. If you think I'll ever send my Son again, forget it.

Now it is ten o'clock and we are both pretending to sleep. But I can feel his awakeness and probably he can feel mine. I have my radio turned on real low and someone is singing "I'll be home for Christmas" like their heart is breaking wide open. Outside, snow falls, so perfect.

It is with a terrible weariness in my heart that I knock on the door. Mrs. O'Connell opens it. "Well!" she says. *"L'étrangère!* How *are* you, dear?"

"Hello, Mrs. O'Connell, it's nice to see you." I feel like Eddie Haskell on *Leave It to Beaver.*

"Come right in, Cynthia's up in her room. She's been there quite awhile, waiting."

I wipe my feet on the outside rug, step in.

"I wonder..." Mrs. O'Connell says, looking at my shoes with a pained expression. I slip them off, watch her line them up like they are leading the parade. Then I head upstairs, feel her eyes on my back the whole way up.

I sneak a look into Nona's room when I pass by; she's asleep, snoring with her mouth open. I have missed her, that part I always enjoy. Cynthia is on the phone. She holds up a finger to me, then says, "Okay, I have to go. I'll talk to you later."

She hangs up, smiles at me. "Hi!" She doesn't say anything about who was on the phone. Our relationship is at the point where we don't owe things. I have not worn the necklace for over a week. She didn't ask me what was wrong.

I sit in her chair, think how long will I have to be here.

"You wish you hadn't come, huh?"

Well, I didn't mean to show her.

"No!"

She smiles sadly.

"I wanted to come."

She shrugs. "I know it's Taylor, now. But I thought we could still be friends, too."

"We are."

"Not so much."

I am getting a little impatient. "Well, I'm here, Cynthia."

She looks me full in the face like a mother. "No you're not."

"Do you want to do something?"

"Okay," she says. "What?"

Well, she is the hostess.

"Take a walk?" I say.

"Okay."

We head downstairs and Mrs. O'Connell makes a beeline out of the kitchen. "Well! Where are you girls off to?" She always acts like she is being so friendly, but there are things hidden in her voice, like fingers in a fist.

"We're going out for a walk," Cynthia says.

"It's awfully cold."

"I know."

"Well, you certainly *can go,* but it seems to me you'd be more comfortable here. I have a batch of cookies almost ready. Double chocolate chip."

"It's actually pretty nice out," I say. "The sun is warm."

"Isn't that funny, how that works?" Mrs. O'Connell says, smiling. "That it can feel so warm when it's not?"

"I'm going out, Mom," Cynthia says.

" 'Bye, now," I say, in a way I know Taylor would love.

"Well, all right then, I'll see you in about fifteen minutes, how's that?" she says, as we walk down the steps. "I'll just go get your plates ready. Now. Cocoa or cold milk?"

Neither of us says a word. I am proud of Cynthia. This is the time of growing up for all of us. I can see it in my body, too. Last night I lay in the bathtub looking at my legs. These new ones are longer. The knees are more square and horsey. They are not my old legs. Those old ones are gone.

I am spending all Saturday with Taylor, and the night, too. That is how good an impression she made on my father. The most unbelievable thing is she made him laugh. Twice! Taylor is like a slinky chameleon, deciding what a person needs and then changing into it. She acted like being in the army was like being president. She asked him a million questions. Ginger was there, and I could feel her eyes on me, *Katie?* I didn't look up. I let Taylor do all the work, and I just ate. To tell the truth, I really enjoyed it. It was relaxing. I thought, When did I ever before feel this way at my dinner table? The answer was, never.

This afternoon, we are going out shopping with Gwen. I told Taylor no stealing and she said fine, she'd pay for things, it didn't matter either way. We are a few blocks from the house when Taylor says, "Let me drive."

"You want to?" Gwen asks.

"You can drive?" I say.

Taylor turns around to look at me in the backseat. "Can't you?"

"I've never tried."

"It's easy."

"You want to try?" Gwen's laughing eyes in the rear view. They're doing Fun With Katie.

"Yeah," I say.

That ought to stop them.

But Gwen pulls over, gets out of the car, comes around to sit in the back. "Go ahead," she tells me.

I sit there, saying nothing.

"Go!"

"Come on," Taylor says. "I'll teach you."

I get out of the backseat, come around front, slide behind the steering wheel. I put my hands on it. Oh, the feeling. I am right now in that TV commercial, "See the USA in your Chevrolet." I lean back against the seat, look into the rearview, then the sideview mirrors. Everything looks weird and backward and scary.

"I don't want to," I say, and start to get out.

"Just put it in drive," Taylor says. "Put your foot on the brake first."

I look down at the pedals, point. "This one?"

"Maybe she shouldn't do this," Gwen says.

"Relax, I'll watch her." In their relationship, Taylor acts like she's the older one.

"Put your foot on the brake first, and then put it in drive."

I look around. We're on a deserted suburban street. No one is out. I put my foot on the brake. The car grows fifty times bigger.

"Now put it in drive," Taylor says. "Move that red line to the *D*."

I pull the stick down, feel a little clunk, jump. Well, now, there. I have broken the car. I look over at Taylor, sick. How will I pay?

"What, you're doing fine!" says.

Oh. I breathe out, get re-excited.

"Now just press down gently on the accelerator," Taylor says. "That other pedal."

"Okay." I push down and suddenly we are going across someone's front lawn and everyone is screaming.

"Stop!" Taylor yells. "Put your foot on the brake!" I do, and Taylor goes flying onto the floor. I look at her, scared she is bad hurt, but she is only laughing, holding her head. Gwen is laughing, too. And then so am I. "Put it in park," Taylor says, *"P."*

I do, like an expert if I do say so myself.

"And get out." She is still laughing. She opens her car door and starts for my side. I get out, too, head for the backseat.

"No, just stay up there with Taylor," Gwen says. "The two of you belong together."

Well. I think I am flattered.

Taylor drives slowly off the lawn, bumps down the curb. There are bad tire tracks all over the place.

"They'll go away," Taylor says, seeing me look back at them. "By tonight, they'll be gone." I don't know if that's true. But she knows more about cars than I do. And anyway, there's nothing I can do about it now.

Taylor drives all the way to the store. She does everything right. Once, a police car pulls up behind us. "Cop," Gwen says. "Watch it." Taylor looks into the rearview mirror, smiles. I look slowly behind me. The cop is smiling back. And then we lose him without even trying.

Dear Katie,

Happy New Year! Well, I knew a trip could restore my spirits to a high note and once your spirits are right everything can change for the better. To make a long story short, who's sorry now? I am back in school and with someone altogether different, Ed Lombrowsky, which I never noticed him before, but boy I should have. And I have been nominated for yearbook queen. As you know I am only a junior and that honor usually falls to a senior. I feel like I have awakened from a bad dream. Thank you for being such a good hostess to me in my time of need. The only thing that was not good was meeting you know who, as if you didn't know. I am not jealous to say this, Katie, but I don't think she is a good friend for you. Don't ask me how I know. I can just tell.

I told my mother about Jimmy, don't get mad! But I was so excited that you have an A+ boyfriend. He has eyes like that Paul Newman. In fact I personally would say that he is better looking than Paul Newman, which is how serious I am that he is A+. Remember what I told you and victory is near. And also remember about when you walk through a storm you see a golden sky.

I have to tell you something. My mother is what they call going through the change. How I found out is we were all of a sudden out of Kotex. Not a one. And I had to tell her to buy some. This never happened before. And then I saw how only I am using it. And she has been off sitting by herself which you know very well is not *my mother. It must be a sorrow that her days of being a woman are over. But what can you do? Well, my father has been extra nice, I'll tell you that. Which might help make up for Bubba, who has been his usual self. Today he came home from school and ate an entire steak for a snack that was for the whole family to eat for dinner. I pity the girl who ends up with him.*

I hope you can come this summer. Ask your dad when he's in a good mood can you come just for a week. Anyway do you miss Texas?

I am now being called to dinner. Which is probably two grains of rice and a pea because Bubba ate everything else.

I hope everything is going well for you. Whew! is mostly what I have to say about me!

Write back, duck, or you'll have bad luck. I just made that up now. Duck *is a word of affection in London, England, did you know that?*

Love,

Cherylanne

There is everything wrong with New Year's resolutions. First, you make a list that is plain impossible because you are in such a good mood thinking you can turn over a new leaf just like that, just because the ball drops. Then you have to watch as each one does not work out, which makes you very disappointed and discouraged, which is the opposite of what the resolutions are supposed to do. I had down to lose weight, one. But all that has happened is I have *gained.* I got on the scale and saw the number and wanted to punch it. But it is my fault. And Ginger's. I am getting some Metrecal.

Next was to dress better, which you cannot do if your clothes are still the same thing on January 1 and your father says, What for? when you say you need more.

Third, I have gotten nowhere fast with Jimmy. I visit him and he thinks, What a nice kid when I walk away instead of Oh, in my heart is a secret love and soon we will be together. Well, there is one thing, which is that I said to him on January 3rd, "The fifty-four Jaguar had a double overhead camshaft unit." He looked at me like he didn't quite know what to think about what he'd just heard. Then, quick, before he could ask any questions like "You know what a *cam*shaft is?" I said, "Of course it wasn't that much more powerful than the Corvette engine, only smoother." "That's right!" he said, smiling broadly, and he was so happy he forgot to think about whether I really knew what I was talking about. Which I of course did not. I found that stuff in a library book, memorized it like French vocabulary. Later when I have time I will find out what everything means for real. I would be willing to take a summer class in cars. But anyway my saying this about Jaguars did not really bring us closer. I would say in the end it was a failure.

The one and only resolution I have lived up to is to be nicer to Cynthia. I went to see her last week and we actually had a good time and it made me see that you can have more than one friend in your life, and ones of many kinds, it is just a matter of scheduling. Nona is bad sick, even her voice is weak. She can't yell at her daughter anymore and I think this is the thing she liked most in life since her husband died. I sat on a chair by her bed for awhile, I'd brought her a Hallmark card. I asked, How are you feeling? though it was plain to see the answer without her saying a word. "I'm-a death warm over," she said. And then she said, "Well, whattya gon' do, go complain-a city hall?" She is so funny even when she is sad. I have taken to writing down certain things that she says. She has a bucking-bronco spirit that I think Cynthia will inherit. It seems that as Nona fades, Cynthia gets brighter. Naturally her mother is fit to be tied. She is going around with her vacuum rubbing those carpets hard, thinking, How can I get that girl back under my thumb. But Cynthia is not going back to that old place, you can see it. She hung a picture from *Photoplay* on her wall with Scotch tape, Sandra Dee. When her mother said, Well now, Cynthia, do you remember what tape does to the wall? Cynthia hung up another one! Actually, it was Cynthia's New Year's resolution to ignore her mother when she acts crazy, which is about 90 percent of the time. I have to admit that I helped a little with this resolution, but it was already just lying in Cynthia waiting to get born. And Cynthia is doing just what she promised she would.

But not me. I started out grand but now I feel like I am just sitting at an empty desk, fingers drumming and drumming. And also nervous, like I am about to explode.

Today is the day. He is getting stuffed angel cake. I cut a generous piece, put it smack dead center on a nice paper plate, silver foil over it. I was going to tape a pretty picture from a magazine on top of the foil, but it doesn't pay to push too hard.

The walk to the station is nice today. The sky is full of puffy kinds of clouds that don't seem to go with winter, but there they are. It is bright enough to wear sunglasses, which I don't have. When Cherylanne was here she advised me to get some because they add a sex appeal. But I don't know. When I wear a hat or sunglasses I feel stupid. Same thing with nail polish. I am more a plain type.

Jimmy is not in his office, and I don't see him outside either. I put the cake on his desk, go to look for him in the garage. And there he is, sitting in his Corvette. The top is down. It looks nicer with the top down. You want to get in.

"Hey," I say.

He startles, which makes me feel so tender toward him like he is a little boy.

"Sorry," I say. "It's just me."

"Is anyone else out there?"

"No. But guess what, I brought you a surprise."

He climbs out of the car, closes the door as

though it were made of glass. Well, Corvettes *are* made of Fiberglas, he told me, and I said, Uh-huh, I see, even though it seemed like a stupid idea to me to make a car out of glass. He stands looking at the car for awhile, and then he looks over at me. "Hey, Katie," he says. There is mystery fun in his voice. Diane used to sound like this sometimes before she did bad things. Well, dangerous things. Sometimes it comes like a pinch to the heart how I miss her. Letters are not the same as when you are hip to hip watching television in the gray light and sharing a box of Good & Plenty. Plus one thing Diane does not like is writing letters or anything else.

"Want to go for a ride?"

"Me?" I say, pointing to myself. I wish, I wish, I wish I would stop this, but it comes out like a hiccup and there you are, it is too late.

"Yeah. You."

"Well... It's still winter."

"I know."

"It's pretty slushy."

"I'll wash it after. You can help, if you want."

"Sure!" I feel like a happy dog, who goes nuts just because you say the word *walk*. But Jimmy would not let just anyone touch his car, I know it for a fact. This is a real step up the ladder.

Jimmy goes out front to put a note on the door and lock up. Then he comes back into the garage, smiling, his jacket on and zipped high. "Button up," he says, pointing with his chin to my collar.

He takes care of you, it is in his nature. If he came to a dying flower dropped on the street he would still move it so it wouldn't get stepped on. I button the top button of my coat, which chokes me to death but who cares.

"Okay!" He opens my door for me like the coachman for Cinderella herself. Then the garage door opens, and we back out slowly. The sound of the engine is so cute and mumbly. He puts it into gear and we take off. We are way low to the ground. I love this car. It is so bright on the inside like lipstick. I wish I could watch us from the outside, going down the road together.

It's cold with the top down, but it's fun, too. The heater will not exactly win any awards, but when you know in a little while you'll be warm again, you're all right. I love the sight of Jimmy's profile, his bare hands on the wheel. The wind is whipping his hair around, his ears are bright red. We go up and down streets, turn left, turn right, go wherever we want. People look at us, especially men. The women look like, Oh isn't that cute, but the men stop and stare till we're gone and I would bet one million dollars I know what they're thinking, which is, Boy, I wish I had one, I want one too. Yes, I say back a little snobby, it's a '54 Corvette, it's a Blue Flame 6. When we head back to the garage, I am disappointed. I know he has to work, but I wish we could stay out till the sun went down and then some.

The garage door shuts, and I climb out of the car, close the door gently, push my hair out of my face. I feel like I've been on a good ride in an amusement park. Exhilarated, and a little out of breath. Jimmy sits behind the wheel saying nothing. He doesn't look like he feels the same way. Finally he gets out, grabs a rag, throws one to me. "I'll just get a bucket," he says. Something is wrong. His walk is too heavy.

"Want me to take the sign down off the door?" I ask.

"Oh, man, I forgot. Yeah, would you? Thank you. Unlock it, too, okay? Keys are in the door."

While I'm in the office, I dump old coffee out of his cup, then wash and dry it. I put it upside down on his desk so he'll know it's ready to go. This is something I've seen in restaurants and it always made sense to me. I straighten his books and papers, line his chair up even with his desk. I take the broom and give the floor a little sweep. This is all the house we have for now.

Finally, I take the foil off the cake. And now my flying spirits take a dive. The whipped cream is all thinned out and melting. The cake doesn't look delicious at all. It looks like garbage, the kind you don't want to pick up because it will give you the willies to touch it. The pretty colors it used to have, a red-pink mixed with white, have now blended together to look like an accident. It's is a good thing I got here first or Jimmy would think, That girl is not ready for anything. I throw the cake in the garbage. Well, you would think they would say something in the recipe about this, do not leave out too long.

When I go back into the garage, Jimmy is done with his side of the car and starting on mine. "I got it," he says. "I'm almost done."

He finishes, stands up and stares at the car again, one hand on his hip. Watching him, I feel as though I can see the car with his eyes: its smooth, rounded lines, its tires with their whitewalls and red stripe and decorated hubcaps, its shiny dashboard dials lined up neat, the little wing off the taillight just to be fancy. It reminds me of when you watch a person who knows a lot about music listen to a record, how they close their eyes like they're in a good kind of pain, and all of a sudden you hear things you never heard before, just from the love way they move their eyebrows. Oh, you think. I get it.

Jimmy sighs. "Well, say good-bye to it."

"To the car? Why?"

"I'm selling it."

"Why?"

He walks past me into his office, slumps into his desk chair. "My wife found out about it. We really can't afford it. She's right, I never should have bought it. Guy's coming tonight to pick it up."

"But you really like it."

"I know. But it was wrong. I shouldn't have kept it from her, that I had it."

"Jimmy?"

"Yeah."

"I think you should keep that car."

"I know you do."

The bells rings, and he gets up to take care of a pickup truck, which takes about a hundred years, I hate when trucks come. "How you doing?" I hear him say friendly to the driver, even though his heart is plumb breaking. I watch him, my forehead up against the glass. I will someday buy him two Corvettes. One exactly like the one he is selling and one of whatever else he wants. "Go ahead," I'll say, waving my arm out over a sea of Corvettes. "Pick whatever you want." "Katie!" he'll say. Although by that time it will be Katherine. "Katherine!" he'll say. "No," I'll say. "I mean it." "Well, all right," he'll say, "but then *I'm* going to buy *you* something." "Never mind," I will say. "I don't need a thing."

When Jimmy comes in, he is different. "Tell you what," he says. "After I get the money, I'll take you out for a Coke. Hell, I'll take you out for a whole dinner."

Well, look what has dropped right here.

"I... Okay." I always thought it might happen when I was not expecting it, that it would all of a sudden just be here. I will wear something very simple, but tasteful. A whole dress, not a skirt and sweater. The pearl earrings, of course. I will order something easy to eat and with no garlic. Diane told me shrimp was good, fried shrimp, you can just daintily pick it up, give a little dip in the catsup and put it quietly in your mouth. We will have a long, serious talk. "It's all right," I will say about how guilty he feels about leaving his wife.

"You didn't plan it." I will put my hand lightly over his, *I am here for you.* I have to get some lotion.

"I should tell you, too... I'm going to be moving."

"When?" Things are going fast. He is getting his own place, which will have things like only two towels and he will have to make scrambled eggs in a pot.

"In about three weeks."

"Where?" Maybe close to my house!

"Up to Iowa. My wife has a brother there, willing to hire me. He'd pay more than I can make here."

Oh, now, No. No.

He is looking at me like he expects me to say something.

"Well... do you like Iowa?" I ask.

Where is Iowa? Where is Iowa? How far?

"I don't know," he says.

I know that feeling, of moving somewhere you know nothing about, where you don't really want to go.

I am in a kind of panic. He is looking down in the defeated way. His eyelashes make little shadows on his cheeks. He is a beautiful man, fit to be used as a model for the artist Michelangelo. I don't think he has any idea. And now he is leaving.

"You are a very handsome man." My voice is wearing boots and marching.

He looks up, smiles. "Well, thank you. And you are a very attractive young lady."

"I think I love you."

His look freezes.

"No. I do. I can tell."

"Oh, Katie. I didn't know... I didn't mean to—"

"You didn't do it. You didn't do it. It just happened by its own self."

We stare at each other, still as stone. And then I leave. I walk home somehow. Somehow, I do. On the way I am thinking, he loves his wife. He wants so much to please her. He will do anything to please her. He told me that she was in love with his best friend, Chris, who broke up with her when they were all seniors in high school, and she went out with Jimmy just to get back at Chris. She did everything with Jimmy to get back at Chris. At the time I thought Jimmy was saying, See how I got roped in? But he wasn't saying that. He was saying God, I love her, I wish she loved me. I didn't want to see that then, but I see it now. It was in his voice every time he talked to her on the phone. It was in the way I saw him kissing her. His love is pure and direct and longing and the beam goes straight to her. As mine goes to him. I think, all in the whole world, there are just lines of people with the one in front never turning to see the one behind, and the one behind too shy to give a small tap on the shoulder. Well, at least I did that. At least I told.

Ginger knocks at my door.

"Not now," I say.

She doesn't come in, but she doesn't go away.

I raise my head off the pillow. It is heavy with

the snot of crying. "Not *NOW!*" I say.

I hear her walk away. There is a slice of me saying, Oh now don't. The rest of me is saying, Who cares when I know now, I can't ever see him again. And he was the one. He was. It is the truest thing about me. It will never change. When I am fifty, I will say fast and automatic, "Jimmy."

I clear my throat so Mr. Spurlock will look up from his newspaper and see my raised hand.

"Yes, Katie?"

"I can't read what you wrote."

He stands up, walks over to his chicken scratches on the blackboard. "Which part?"

I am really so sick of him and his half-bald head, which he tries to disguise by combing long sides over the top, but it does not work at all because the sides slip down. Mostly he looks like Clarabelle.

"See the first line?"

"Yes, that says, 'The New Deal—' "

"No," I say. "I mean, if you take the first line and go all the way to the last line, that is what I can't read."

He stands there, blinking. He reminds of a chimpanzee I once caught the glance of. We stood there staring at each other. "Yes?" we were both thinking.

"So what you are saying, Katie, is that you can't read any of this."

"Yes, sir."

A king-sized miracle has happened. The students in Mr. Spurlock's class are sitting up, interested and alert.

"Well, do you need glasses?"

"No. A teacher would do."

"Pardon *me*, young lady?"
I say loudly, "I said, 'A *teacher* would do.' All you are is a newspaper reader. You don't teach anything. All you do is put Sanskrit on the board."
He is not listening. He is over at his desk writing out the hall pass. Guess where I am going. Well, bingo, it's exactly what I wanted.

"Your school called," Ginger says, when I get home.
I say nothing, head out to the kitchen to fix a snack.
In a minute, she comes in, leans against the doorjamb, watching me. "I said that I would take responsibility for relaying the message to your father."
I pour a glass of milk, sit at the table, bite into my sandwich.
"You got sent to the principal?"
I chew and chew.
"For talking back to a teacher?"
Peanut-butter and jelly. It's good.
"Katie?"
"What?"
"You want to tell me what happened?"
"If you want to tell my father, tell my father."
"I won't tell your father."
I stare at her and my eyes start to cry, which is very odd since my insides are stone-cold concrete and do not care about one single thing.
"You want to talk, honey? You want to tell me?"

I nod, my throat gulping like a bullfrog.

It is midnight and I am not even faintly tired. I am sitting at the window in my desk chair, wide awake and looking out at nothing. If I were a man I would go out right now and get a big bottle of whiskey and sit in a chair with my legs stuck out straight and get good and stinking drunk. I sigh, lean forward, put my elbows on the windowsill. There's a little draft leaking through, the cold feels good against my face.

Ginger was so nice. It seemed for awhile like her heart was breaking right with mine. But then she said there would be others. And she said you never know, you just never know when you will meet them. She said that the men she had cared most for in her life, why, it had been an accident that she met them. One she met taking out the garbage! At first I thought she meant she'd loved a garbage man, which I guess is fine, but she said, Oh no Stanley was walking his dog and I was taking out the garbage. What happened to Stanley I asked and she said, Well it just didn't work out, which I guess means he dumped her. She said you wait, you'll see, there is not just one person in the world to love, it would be terrible if that were true. I did not nod yes. I just don't know. Life is full of surprises, Ginger said. That's what makes it fun.

I hear a yowling noise and see a cat at the door of Greg and Marsha's house. I didn't know they had a cat. I think, well, there is a surprise right there. Maybe this is a sign that she's right.

I am sitting in my room, ready for date number two. Double date number two. This time, Taylor and the boys are coming to the house to pick me up. It is Michael again, so I did not make him puke so bad after all and Taylor has told him none of that attack stuff anymore. We are going to eat. I don't really know why you make a whole date out of eating, but everyone does. We are going to a place called Steak and Shake. You get the onion rings and the steak burger. It's a hangout for kids who go to schools other than mine. Better kids, Taylor said. I got my makeup on just right, probably because I don't really care how it goes on, this evening is not that.

The doorbell rings, and I go out into the living room, introduce everyone. My father is not so bad. Not that he smiles or anything, but when Michael calls him Mr. he does not say, *"Colonel."* But I know he is thinking it. You can tell by the way he feels his keys in his pocket that he is holding his rearing self back. "Be home on time," he tells me.

"I know."

"Have her back here on time," he tells Michael.

Well, what does he think, we are deaf?

"Hey," Taylor says. "Why don't *you* come?"

My father looks at her, smiles, shuts the door. She has a power, Taylor. She can snip the line, just like that.

Well, this is it. The end of Taylor and me, because I cannot trust her. We are all of us in a dark place with no houses around. I would say we are not here to play canasta. No, we are parking. We have forty minutes before I have to be home. What better thing to do than to park? is what these three are thinking.

"There was a young lady named Sinn," John says.

"Shut up, John," Taylor says.

"Who said 'Let us do it again,' " he continues.

"Shut *up!*" Taylor looks quick at me, then back at him.

" 'And again, and again, and again and again—' "

"Fuck you," she says, and her head goes below the seat with his.

I look out the window, see my own eyeliner face looking back. I have chosen door number one and the audience is saying "Awwwwwww!" Yes, this is the end of Taylor and me.

Michael puts his hand on my shoulder. I kiss him for something to do.

In awhile, he starts touching me again. "No," I say.

"All right, little girl," he whispers. "I won't touch you. Why don't you touch me."

I swear I can feel my dinner rising in my throat.

"Here," he says. "It's nice." And he takes my hand and he puts it down his pants to a pile of weird flesh like the insides of a chicken. I yank my hand out and use it to slap him. I don't care. I don't care. I don't care.

I am back at the pond because it was my place first and it still belongs to me. And it still is a soothing place, beautiful and safe, not saying anything about anything.

The water is dark blue and cold-looking, ice only in rare spots at the edges. I look up at the Mobil station only once, to see if he is looking, which he is not.

I use a stick to dig a hole in the earth, think, this is where the sadness goes. I dig it as deep as I can, then cover it up. I wave my hand over it, a slow circle. When I stand up, I check to see if it worked. Nope. My whole self is still heavy.

I bring the stick back with me, use it to touch various things along the way. Magic. "There," I whisper in my fairy voice to a fence post, a street sign. "There!" It is odd how when you feel like you have nothing, you can act like you have everything.

I am at Nona's funeral, sitting by Cynthia. I didn't want to come, but it must be the height of rudeness to say no to an invitation like that. "Will you come to my grandmother's funeral?" "Oh, sorry, I'm going bowling."

Mrs. O'Connell is actually quiet. She nodded at me when my father dropped me off at their house and that is it. She said nothing in the car on the way over. She is wearing a black outfit and a hat with a black veil. You can see diamond-shaped pieces of her grieving face. This is the first time I've met Cynthia's father. He looks jolly, like he works in a candy store, but he doesn't, he's a banker.

Cynthia has not cried, but she is so pale I'm afraid she's going to faint. Nona is the star of the show, of course, lying up there in the open coffin, a rosary wrapped around her hands. It's a pearly pink rosary with a gold crucifix, very pretty. I knelt by her when it was my turn in the reception line before the service started, and she looked so real. She looked like she was breathing, but of course that always happens, it's just your own self moving and you transfer it over. Even looking at Nona lying in a coffin, I couldn't believe such a fiery person was dead. They put makeup on her and did her hair puffed up. She looks real, but she doesn't look normal. They should have buried her in an apron, surrounded her with spaghetti and tomatoes and garlic. Like the Egyptians, send her off with what she loves. I'll tell you one thing, I never saw Nona with a rosary in her hands. I told Cynthia that and she said yes but Nona was very religious, she used to be the president of the Santa Lucia Society. "She kept the banner in her room for a long time," Cynthia said. "It had a picture of St. Lucy with her eyes plucked out."

"Why?" I asked. I couldn't believe it. Why would someone make a whole banner out of something like that. "Oh, Mrs. Whatever, your daughter has had her eyes plucked out!" "Oh no, well, let's make a banner out of it!" Cynthia said St. Lucy's eyes got plucked out because she was a virgin martyr. I have no idea what that means. Those Catholics have strange stories and they love those pictures that make you practically puke. Jesus with His heart all stuck out, for one. And nailed up on the cross, dribbles of blood running down so sickening you can hardly even feel sorry for Him. As if His mother, who was right there, wouldn't have wiped it off.

"Nona used to be really active in the church," Cynthia said. "People were all the time calling her or she was calling them. She had a phone caddy, you know, one of those flip-up ones, you put the arrow to the letter you want and it flips up? She had one of those, gold metal, and she used to lie in bed at night with that phone caddy talking in Italian real loud."

She smiled and then she looked sad because she remembered that this is it for Nona, no more phone calls, ever. I didn't ask any more questions. It wasn't really right of me to be acting like Brenda Starr, reporter. I was just there to be a friend to Cynthia in her time of sorrow. She listened to me when I told her about Jimmy. I told her and Cherylanne, but not Taylor. I thought Taylor would say, "Big deal. There's more where that came from." And that is so not true.

The priest begins his sorrowful speech about Nona's life. Mrs. O'Connell starts to cry real hard and there are tears rolling down Cynthia's cheeks. I bite my lips a little, stare straight ahead. Under my shirt is my half of the best-friends necklace. I'm sorry I ever took it off. It offers something to you to have one of those.

"Nona died," I tell Father Compton.

"I'm sorry to hear that. She was a friend of yours, really, wasn't she?"

"Yes."

"Hard to loose two friends at once."

"Well, Jimmy was not my friend." Now I am pure sorry I told him about Jimmy. He nodded all sympathetic but I can see that he did not really understand, either.

I look right at him. "He was not my friend. I loved him."

"I know you did."

"No, see, you say that but what you are thinking is, puppy love."

"No. No, I am not. I am thinking that in the best kinds of love there is friendship, too."

Well, that is true. He has said a true thing and I have yelled at him for nothing.

"I'm sorry," I say.

"It's all right."

"Maybe I'll come to Mass this Sunday."

His eyes change, but he says nothing.

"When is it?"

"I say the seven-thirty and the eleven o'clock."

"Well, seven-thirty is no good."

"Uh-huh."

Nothing more. These Catholics are good, I have to hand it to them.

Oh, all right, I think, but I don't say anything. This way it's not a promise.

On the way home, I think, Wait. Maybe he meant Taylor when he said that about losing two friends and then I just dove into Jimmy and he didn't say one word. Because he saw my need. He said silently, Well all right, child, that's fine. I have piled up inside me quite a bit of gratefulness for him.

Maybe Mass is interesting. I know one thing is they actually believe the priest is standing there with the host and, presto, it becomes Jesus Himself. And then they eat Him.

Well, now here I am in my room with nothing to do again. Things have come back to that. It is Sunday and Cynthia is off with relatives. When someone dies, all you do for about a week is spend time with relatives and eat.

Taylor called, did I want to come over? but she has just worn me out. I would like to think that sometime we could be friends again, but I don't know. I think it was because of her that I stole this lipstick sample last week. I know it's not as bad as what she does, but still. It's crème caramel, a pretty light brown color. I keep it in my underwear drawer and every time I wear it it is a thrill. So I can see how I could move up on the stealing line. One day Taylor showed me some things she stole, shoes, records, books. And the next time I was in a department store I was looking at purses and I realized I could just put one over my shoulder and walk out. They would not catch me, I knew it. I got all dry in the mouth and trembly, like, okay, let's go, do it. But I didn't, I walked away. Taylor is a funny person who doesn't see any right and any wrong and it is too strong to be around. I suppose someday she will be famous and people will say, "You quit hanging around with *her? Why???*" and I will say there is more to it than I can explain.

I wrote to Diane this morning, even though she still has not sent me anything but a postcard saying she is moving to California. She didn't say she and Dickie. I asked her in my letter, is he going with you or are you getting a divorce? Although I already know the answer. Their marriage was a little paper boat in the gutter that only sailed because there was a storm. Now that it is calm, Diane is looking at Dickie and saying never mind. And poor Dickie.

Well what else is new, in the world of love, things never work out even. Even when people think they are even, they are not. Take my father and Ginger, who it looks like any day now are going to tell me they're getting married and I will say, No kidding I have only known for about two hundred years. Ginger is the one who loves more. Even though my father has a great deal of affection for her, she loves more than he does.

I have heard them at night in the living room. Ginger is worried about how will I feel, which is so nice of her but really it is not to do with me and I am already used to it, big deal.

I stand up, do some toe touches. I am too fat to be a teenager. Although it does not matter, because I am done with the dating game. I met the one and he is gone. I guess he really is gone, now, too, three weeks are up. I know all my life no one will believe the trueness of this, that he was the only one for me. I saw everything about him. He was a tender man and so handsome you could die. You could say anything to him. He was interested in me, he thought I was interesting. Around him, everything bad about me was excused and everything good about me got held up. I have been on this earth long enough to know how hard it is to find all that in a man and I know I will never find it again and even if an exact copy of Jimmy came to me later like when I was twenty-three, no, it would not be right. Sometimes you just know things even though you are at a young age, and believe me, I do know. But from now on I will keep it to myself. People don't believe you. I saw how Ginger tried to listen and believe me but behind her eyes she was making plans for me that I am not one bit interested in. I mean love plans, like who could be next. Well, I do not need love, I am just going to be a poet.

I go into the living room, stare out the front window. Not one fun thing to look at. I have no idea why they have to make every single house look just the same. Why not build a house around a tree, so that smack in the middle of your living room, nature. Why not have round windows and crazy angle ones, walls of glass, rainbow colors painted everywhere? My house will have that. I will draw how it should go and they will build it and say, My, I never *thought* of that!

Ginger and my father are out buying lamps for the house. Give me a break that I'm not supposed to know they're getting married. You would have to be an imbecile not to see that. Well, I'll get to have Bones. Me and Bridgette, she'll have a stepbrother.

I put on my coat. Sometimes when I do this I figure out where I want to go.

The pond.

I get some pieces of bread for the ducks, step outside. The snow is all gone. Now, with the sky for the ceiling, I am already better. They ought to let crazy people outside. It would help.

This is my lucky day, there is a duck convention. I sit with my back to the station. I don't want any memories to wreck how green the males' feathers are. I throw a few crumbs and the ducks come swimming over, quacking away. I wonder if they are saying, Oh boy, bread, or Get the hell out of my way. Some stay in the water and others waddle onto the shore. I should have brought more bread. There aren't a whole lot of things much finer in life than feeding ducks and now I will run out too soon.

"Hi," I hear.

I quick turn around and it's a good thing I'm sitting down. He is not gone. He is right here. Right there. How long?

"Hi, Jimmy."

He walks the rest of the way toward me. "I'm glad to see you."

"...Oh."

"Can we talk a little?"

"I thought you were moving."

"I am. Today's my last day. I just got off work and saw you sitting down here."

"I'm feeding the ducks."

"Yeah, I see."

"I thought you were gone."

"Took a little longer than we thought."

He sits down, puts his arms on his knees, looks out at the water. "Pretty out, today. Not so cold."

One thing I do not need is the weather report. Plus looking at him is making me feel like crying. I stand up, brush the crumbs off my coat.

"Well, nice to see you, I have to go."

He looks up at me.

"See you," I say.

"Katie? Could you spare a minute? There are some things I really want to say to you."

I think of two fists, only one holding something. Pick.

I sit back down, don't look at him. But I can smell him. It is not cologne smell, it is just soap-and-water smell and it practically kills me dead.

He takes in a breath, starts to say something, then stops. "Dang," he says quietly.

Inside, the tight bud of my heart starts to open again.

"Well, look. I just want to tell you that I'm so... honored that you cared for me, Katie."

Here, the sting of tears. The body drives, the mind comes along.

"That's okay."

"No. You are such a fine person, and you know what? You're just going to get better and better. Some day, when you are ready, some man is going to love you so much."

Well here comes the flood. I am crying and crying and crying. "I don't want anyone else," I say. "I am finished. I only wanted you. You are just the right one and there will never be—" I look at him fiercely. "I went out with someone else. And all he did was shove my hand down his pants!"

I cannot believe I have said this. Jimmy is shocked. Well, what else can he be.

I look down, wipe the tears from my face, draw a defiant *X* in the dirt.

A raggedy silence.

And then he says so gentle, "Katie?"

How he says it is how I can look up at him.

"I wish I could tell you. You know, when it happens that you really love someone—I know you think you won't, I know you believe you will always love me, and Katie, I would be so happy to think that in some way you will, but you will love someone else again, too."

"Nope," I say. "I will not."

"Listen to me," he says. "I want to tell you something. Boys... aren't like girls. Boys will do things like you told me because they don't care or they don't know... lots of stupid reasons. It doesn't have to do with you. It has to do with them. But I want you to hold out for something I know will come to you. And I think maybe you know it, too."

I don't look, but I listen so hard.

"When you have sex the real way, the way it's supposed to be, it's like... Well, it's like taking and giving at the same time. It's this fierce thing, it's... God, it's like your whole soul gets snatched away from you and then returned, better."

"That's what you have, huh?" I say, miserably.

"And that's what you'll have, too. Someday."

I look out at the ducks, most of them given up and gone now, but a few hanging around, just in case.

It comes to me that when you get right down to it, I am not that crazy about youth.

"I wish you'd believe me," Jimmy says.

"I don't care," I say.

"You don't care?"

"No, I don't care about one thing."

He frowns. "Well, Katie, I—"

I stand up. "I have to go."

He stands too. "No, you don't. I'll go."

He takes off his glove, offers me his bare hand. "Good-bye, Katie. I enjoyed so much having you for a friend. More than you know."

I look at his square nails, the small wound at the side of his thumb, no Band-Aid. I want, my insides are saying. I want. I want.

I don't take his hand. "Just go," I say, cold.

He nods, puts his glove back on, turns to walk away and I can't stand it. I call his name, run over to him. He catches me in his arms so gently and the fit is just right. I look up at him and ask him with all of me to just kiss me once, just once. He leans down and there, light as a butterfly, his lips on my forehead.

No. Not that way. I don't move.

He sighs, smiles, pulls off his glove to put his hand to my face. There, the backs of his fingers, moving up my cheek so light it gives me the chills. And then he turns and walks away.

I watch him get into his car, drive down the road away from me. I don't even have a picture of him. I feel a bad ache rising up in me like an inside monster. And I have had some hard moments already. The other day I was thinking about Jimmy while I was fixing toast. I was looking at the deep red of the jelly and in my head came this little play about how I would cut my wrists and die. It seemed so real. It is why I told Father Compton everything.

I had to tell someone. I was sort of scared. And we talked a long time about sadness. He said, Well Katie, there was your mother and a move and then Jimmy. I said yeah. He said these were important events in my life and sorrow was a funny thing. I said I didn't think sorrow was so funny. He said no what he meant was that it could teach you about joy. I said is that right. He said yes. He said not to be afraid of sorrow, really, that it was just a kind of teacher. A bad teacher, I said. Father Compton said, Well now surely I had had experiences with bad teachers in my life, hadn't I? My sad, slow brain actually got revved up for a minute, thinking of that. I said, Are you kidding? This school I'm in now that's their specialty. Father Compton said what he meant was surely I could *survive* a bad teacher. He said there are times we must let sorrow come, learn the lesson and then move on. He said when you think about it, life is just moments. And you have to have faith that the next good moment is coming right along. Then he asked careful was I really thinking about suicide and I said no because then I'd be dead and I wouldn't know how anything turned out. He said, Well there you go, that's exactly right. And then he said that the natural antidote to despair is hope. I said I supposed so and when would I get to that part. He said, Oh you'd be surprised, that from where he sat he could see it already.

Now a cold wind blows suddenly, pushes my hair across my face and I get to see everything in slats. I put my hands deep in my pockets, find Jimmy's stone. I take it out and look at it. It's a very pretty thing, but there are so many people in the world who would just say "Where?" when you told them that.

I put the stone against my face, right where he touched me. And then I fling it far out into the pond. It lands right about where I fell through the ice on the day I met him. I didn't mean to throw it. I wish I hadn't done that. I would like to have that stone back. I could carry it in my pocket no matter where I was or who I was, it would always be there. I could use it like he said, pull it out to soothe a troubled time. I stare out at the closed water, curl my fingers around nothing.

Well, whattya gon' do, go complain-a city hall?

I'm cold. I start for home. Winter will pass. It may seem that it won't, but it will. And that stone isn't leaving, it's just waiting. In the spring, I'll come back and find it again.

ABOUT THE AUTHOR

ELIZABETH BERG's first novel, *Durable Goods,* was called "a gem" by Richard Bausch. *Talk Before Sleep,* which was a 1996 Abby Honor Book, *Range of Motion,* and *The Pull of the Moon* were all critically acclaimed bestsellers. She has published fiction and nonfiction in *Ladies' Home Journal, Good Housekeeping, The New York Times Magazine, Parents,* and *New Woman,* among other places, and has been nominated for a National Magazine Award. She lives in Massachusetts.